A FORCED CONFESSION

Lassiter knew his only chance lay in getting a confession out of Telfont.

Slowly he crept into the parlor to stand where the light was dim, away from the glow of a single lamp. It was on the table where Telfont was scribbling away....

"Careful, Telfont," Lassiter warned in a low voice.

Telfont's shoulders tightened and he straightened up slowly in his chair.

"Well, well, Lassiter," Telfont said with forced cheerfulness. "Guess I must have forgotten to lock the back door." He eyed the shotgun, licked his lips.

"Shut up and listen to me. You've got a man to protect you in this house. Tell him to show himself."

"And if I don't?"

"You'll be a grease spot on that chair."

LOREN ZANE GREY

LASSITER GOLD

LEISURE BOOKS NEW YORK CITY

A LEISURE BOOK®

January 2007

Published by

Dorchester Publishing Co., Inc.
200 Madison Avenue
New York, NY 10016

Copyright © 1986 by Loren Grey
Previously published by Pocket Books.

ISBN 0-8439-5816-2

LASSITER GOLD

CHAPTER ONE

All that day a feeling of doom persisted, coldly plucking Lassiter's backbone like a banjo string. For some weeks he had been working cattle for Xavier Betain and now was on a hurry-up trip with the old man. Xavier drove a team of mules hitched to a battered and dusty wagon. In the bed was a blanket roll and cooking gear. And a brass-bound trunk.

It was the trunk and its possible contents that caused Lassiter to worry about who might be sneaking along their backtrail.

Several times he rode a quarter of a mile or so along this backtrail but saw nothing suspicious. His blue eyes, made all the more penetrating because of his sun-darkened skin, probed the miles of scrub oak and the crumbling sand walls of the deep canyon they traveled. Nothing moved. He was an inch under six feet with strong shoulders and a good length to his legs that suggested power. His black pants and shirt were liberally powdered with dust.

They reached a settlement of dried out buildings

called El Rio, though there wasn't a river for miles. Old man Betain pulled up in front of a combination store and saloon.

"Got to wet my pipes with some drinkin' whiskey," he grinned. "An' I long for the sound of the human voice."

"Just be . . . careful," Lassiter advised as he did each time the old man insisted on pausing for a drink.

"Oh, I will, I will. Next time it'll be your turn."

"I can do without," Lassiter said.

"You keep your eyes on things." And Xavier nodded his white head at the brass-bound trunk and entered the saloon.

Lassiter looked around. A girl with a tired smile leaned in a doorway. But when he failed to show interest, she went back inside. Three trail-worn horses were tied to a hitchrail.

It was nearly an hour before the old man staggered out to the wagon, singing happily under his breath. He might be gray and thinned down, but he was still rawhide tough and with a voice like a bear's roar.

"I trust you, Lassiter," the old man had said before starting the journey. "An' there ain't many men I do trust."

Lassiter had helped drive a herd of Betain's cattle to the Colorado River where buyers from California took over. Then Betain had paid off the crew, retaining only Lassiter. The journey north was to rescue the old man's son. But from what, Lassiter wasn't quite sure yet.

When Lassiter and the old man started north, most of their talks were in the evening. Xavier Betain's fierce eyes reflected the glow of the cook fire. "I done my boy wrong," he'd said. "When I got the ranch, Corse wanted to be a partner. But I wouldn't hear of it. I thought the best way to train a boy was to keep him under the ol' bootheel. Like my pa done me. But now I know it's wrong."

"People change," Lassiter offered, sipping hot coffee.

"Now that he wrote he's in bad trouble, I sold off all my cattle, as you know. I aim to help him." Betain stared at the fire and spoke of his late wife. "A mighty sweet little lady, but strange in her ways. One day she up an' left me an' took my boy. She went to live with her ma. When she died, Corse come back, a growed man. But we couldn't get along. He left."

On this night Lassiter's horse and the hobbled mule team were restless. Lassiter picked up his rifle and put it across his lap and stared hard at the shadows beyond the camp. An occasional shooting star led its flaring tail across the great vaulted ceiling of the night sky.

"Reckon you've guessed what's in the trunk," the old man said with a tight grin.

"More or less."

"Money from the cattle sale. Money for my kid. Although Corse ain't still a kid." Xavier Betain spat into the fire. "Two thousand dollars for you. For helpin' me out."

"So we agreed."

After two long days traversing an almost impassable road through scrub oak and mesquite, past giant slabs of rock that stretched toward the sun, the old man's loose tongue when drinking at El Rio finally stirred up trouble.

In late afternoon they came across a creek alongside the road. It had been a dry day and their canteens were empty. With a yelp of pleasure, Xavier Betain shoved the reins of the mule team into Lassiter's hands and sprang from the wagon.

"Lordy, I'm dry as dust!" he shouted over his shoulder and raced for the creek with his rifle, as fast as his aging legs would allow. There he pawed aside a makeshift fence of brush and tree limbs that surrounded the springs, and flung himself flat. He made great slurping sounds as he sucked water into a parched throat.

Lassiter realized the possible implications of the fence almost too late and shouted a warning. "No, Betain, no . . . !"

And as he started to dismount, he saw a human face peering from behind the thick growth of mesquite directly across the clearing.

"Watch it!" he yelled at the old man. He threw down the reins of the wagon team and drew his .44. At the same moment he rammed in the spurs. His black horse leaped just as a gunshot crashed from the mesquite, and a second bullet from behind came closer to twitch the loosely knotted bandanna around Lassiter's neck. A sound of boots crushing dry brush came from behind him. He pulled savagely on the reins of his hard-running horse. Its head came up, eyes rolling.

A long, sunburned face above a plaid shirt confronted him. The man waved one hand frantically, shouting, "Get at his back, Charlie! His *back!*"

A big Remington revolver roared from the hand of the sunburned man. It hurled a chunk of lead that could have exploded the skull. But Lassiter was bent low over the back of his swerving horse. And as he thundered past, he thumbed two quick shots at the thickest part of the stranger's body.

As he spun his black horse he saw old man Betain sitting up beside the creek in the wreckage of the makeshift fence. Betain held his rifle, aiming it while his body jerked spasmodically. The crack of his rifle was a pure sound above the thunder of hoofbeats from Lassiter's speeding horse.

From the mesquite came a sharp scream. There were the sounds of a man thrashing about. Lassiter hit the ground running. He stumbled, got half a mouthful of sand. From the corner of his eye he saw the old man heaving, as if gripped with convulsions.

But first he had to make sure about the other man, Charlie, get a closer look at that slice of white face he'd glimpsed earlier in the mesquite. He found him, quite dead, tall and rangy and fairly handsome. The old man's bullet had caught him high in the forehead. A long-barreled .45 with ivory handles lay by his outstretched fingers. Lassiter picked it up and hurled it deep into the brush.

Then he hurried to the man with the sunburned face that he had shot. The man was still alive, but moaning. "I .·. I need a doc. . . ."

Lassiter picked up the man's gun and threw it into some oaks.

Out of breath, Lassiter stumbled over to where Betain lay on the ground, heaving.

Grabbing him by the wrists, he pulled the old man away from the creek. Part of the makeshift fence came with him. Only then did Lassiter see the warning that some previous visitor had left on a slab of rock—a skull and crossbones in black paint, and the Spanish word for death, *MUERTE!*

"My God," Lassiter breathed. It confirmed what he had suspected when he'd first seen the fence and shouted a warning at the old man. But at that moment a pair of cutthroats had tried to whipsaw him in a crossfire. Had not Xavier Betain gotten off a lucky rifle shot it might now be Lassiter dead instead of the man Charlie.

Betain groaned. "I'm burnin' up inside . . . my guts is on fire. . . ."

"Likely you drank poisoned water."

"An arsenic spring. Jesus Christ. I . . . I remember there was one along here somewheres, but I plumb forgot about it. . . ." Betain sat with both hands clasped to his belly. Clouds of powdersmoke and dust still wreathed the air. Beads of perspiration dampened the white hair and coursed down the seamed face. "Those bastards were after the trunk, weren't they?"

"Reckon."

"How'd they know about it?" the old man gasped.

"Put two and two together, I guess."

"I . . . I talked to a coupla fellas back at El Rio. . . . Oh, Kee-ryst . . . do you think that was it?" He was stricken again with convulsions.

Lassiter picked him up in his arms. He was surprised at how frail he was. Xavier had given an appearance of reasonably robust health. He got him into the bed of the wagon, then wrapped him in blankets.

He ran to the sunburn-faced man he had shot. "Where's the nearest town?" Lassiter shouted. "I'll see that you get a doctor. . . ."

But the man was dead.

Lassiter's shoulders sagged. "*Cristo*," he muttered.

He went to hunt for the mounts of the two dead men on the chance they might have left behind full canteens. He found them tied off in a clump of scrub oak. But in the air was a film of dust and the sound of rapidly fading hoofbeats. So there had been a third member of the gang.

"Show yourself!" Lassiter yelled, drawing his gun and firing into the air. But whoever it was kept on going, and there was no chance to spot the defector because the ground dipped sharply a hundred yards away. The fugitive would have to be ridden down on horseback and that would take time and Betain needed help.

He found a canteen half full and ran all the way back to Betain. He gave the old man some of the water, holding him up so he could drink. Betain promptly threw it up, and lay back, gasping.

"Money . . . in trunk . . ." Betain rested a trembling hand on the brass-bound trunk. "Gold . . . sixty thousand dollars . . . see that my boy gets it. . . ."

"All right, all right. But first I'm going to get help for you."

Lassiter caught up his black horse and tied it to the tailgate of the wagon.

Then he climbed into the wagon and picked up the reins. "Listen," he said to the old man in the wagon bed, "you know this stretch of country. I don't. Is there a town up ahead? Or do I go back to El Rio?"

"Keep two thousand for yourself, Lassiter. Our original . . . original deal," Betain was saying between groans. Saliva dribbled from his mouth and his eyes were glassy. He caught Lassiter by the wrist with bony fingers that were surprisingly strong. "Your word of honor, Lassiter, that Corse Betain gets that trunk of gold. . . ."

"My word on it."

Then the hand that had reached up to grip his wrist fell away. Betain's head tilted back, his mouth open.

Xavier Betain was dead. Evidently his aging heart had just given out on him. At least the old man had been spared an agonizing death from arsenic poisoning.

Wearily Lassiter stared through slitted eyes at all four points of the compass, hoping to glimpse the third member of the cutthroat outfit.

"Come on, you son of a bitch!" he yelled. But nothing moved.

A search of the old man located a key on a chain. It fit the lock on the trunk. Packed in among some clothing were four leather sacks. Opening them one by one, he saw the glitter of double eagles. Sixty thousand dollars, the old man had said. Fifteen thousand dollars to a sack.

Because he had no idea where the next town might be, he used a short-handled shovel, dug a grave and buried the old man. The dead pair he left where they had fallen. But he did turn their horses loose, along with one of the mules from the wagon team. He took the saddlebags from the horses of the dead renegades and put the treasure into them, then put the saddlebags on the mule's back.

Before leaving, he used an ax from the wagon to cut several thick limbs from the oaks. These he laid across the springs. By the time the next potential drinker started to pull the tree limbs apart, he would see the grim warning painted on the rock. Betain had been in too much of a hurry to notice.

As Lassiter rode out, leading the pack mule, he felt saddened that Xavier Betain hadn't lived to see again the son he had been estranged from for so long. But he would tell the son what had happened, turn over the gold, collect his two thousand dollars, and be on his way. Unless young Betain needed help. Then he'd see. . . .

But his objective now was to reach his destination as soon as possible—the town of Sunrise, far to the north.

A pale-haired girl returned to the scene of the carnage. There was a rip in her boy's shirt and a smudge of dirt on one sun-browned cheek. Her gray eyes reflected fear and hatred.

She had heard the gunshots and the yelling and the sounds of agony made by the gray-haired man. She had come close enough to see the results of the gunshots even though Charlie had warned her to stay away until he and Chick got their hands on the money. Charlie had learned about the money at El Rio.

But each night since El Rio he and Chick had lost their nerve because of the big dark man who acted as Betain's bodyguard and who Chick said was a known killer. She had begged Charlie to give up the mad plan, but he had refused.

Now it was too late. And all because of the black-clad stranger. After Ivy Eading had her spell of weeping over Charlie's body, she hunted for his gun. Finally she located the big ivory-butted .45 that the stranger had thrown into the brush. Although it was too heavy for her to hold in one hand, it would avenge Charlie, the only person in the world who had given one damn about her. Oh, Mrs. Beauchamp down in Tucson had taken her in when the folks had died and let her work a few years in her store, but it wasn't the same kind of caring she'd shared with Charlie.

At El Rio, so Charlie had confided, the old man had let it slip that he and the man known as Lassiter were heading far north to the town of Sunrise. It wasn't all that the old man had let slip that day.

Although the ground was too hard for her to dig graves, Ivy cut brush with the ax left behind and covered the bodies. Then she started out, hat pushed down on rich blond hair and held in place with a chin strap because the wind had come up.

Somewhere to the north was the town of Sunrise. She'd find it.

Every few miles she broke into tears and renewed her vow to settle with Lassiter for murdering poor Charlie Baxter. . . .

CHAPTER TWO

On this spring evening Lassiter was glad he'd buried the money he'd brought north all those dangerous miles. Better to be safe, he had reasoned, than to blunder into unknown possibilities. He had left his mule at the livery barn, then had followed the crowd drifting south out of town toward a large barn. Sitting in his saddle in the shadowy yard, Lassiter overheard the sound of a familiar name.

"Betain," he thought the man had said. But he couldn't be sure because of all the men coming and going in the big yard.

Then he heard another word in connection with Betain. Wake. A wake was being held in the barn. He felt tension across his shoulders.

Lights from two flaring lanterns flanked the wide doorway and threw grotesque shadows across the barn wall. A faint breeze stirred the cottonwoods. There was a hush about the place as if men awaited death's wings. They trooped in and out of the barn.

Grim-faced, some of them, but a few wore secret smiles.

Lassiter felt a cold finger trace the length of his spine. When a barrel of a man with a spike beard strode up from the barn, Lassiter smiled.

"What's inside?" he asked, indicating the barn.

"A wake for Corse Betain," the man said, not noticing the way Lassiter's solid jaw suddenly hardened. "Ain't seen you hereabouts before." The man's speech was slurred.

"Just passing through. Saw the crowd and wondered."

"Wonder no more. Go fetch yourself some drinkin' whiskey. There's plenty of it." The man tittered and stumbled away.

Lassiter's mind spun. He was thinking of the sixty thousand dollars in double eagles that he had buried some three miles west of town, slashing the trunk of a tree with a pocketknife, then going due south some fifty yards and doing likewise to another tree trunk. And the man the money was intended for was now lying dead in the barn.

"Damn poor wake, you ask me," one man muttered to another in passing. "No fiddlers. Etta could afford to hire some, by gad."

"Got what he deserved, Betain did," a woman nearby sniffed. "Him livin' sinful with Etta Dempster. . . ."

The woman passed on with others into deeper shadows.

Lassiter blew out a long-held breath and thought of the impulse that had prompted him to bury the money before coming on to meet Corse Betain face to face.

How fortunate, the way things had turned out. Now what?

Lassiter was to receive two thousand dollars. An agreement sealed with a handshake, Lassiter's strong clasp to that of bony fingers. Two thousand dollars, payment on delivery. That left fifty-eight thousand dollars in double eagles to be delivered to a dead man.

From the barn doorway Lassiter saw some men lift what appeared to be a body and place it in a plain pine casket that rested on two sawhorses.

The man inside the casket was aware of feeble light filtering gradually through the thick lashes of his swollen eyes. An awareness of a flickering of life, shallow breathing, the faint beat of a heart. Where was he? In a box of some kind.

A man said harshly, "Let her see him alone. After all, she was his betrothed."

"Sure, Mr. Telfont, sure." There was a scraping of feet as men moved away from the casket.

It pained the man in the coffin to breathe, to even think. He tried to lift an arm, to signal to the eyes peering in at him. But his limbs were as lifeless as coiled ropes.

The eyes belonged to a young woman with thick black hair and a lace collar at her slender throat. She had a full mouth, and the teeth she bared, whether in agony or some other emotion, were small and even. A handsome woman, he thought.

She was rubbing her eyes, making sounds of sobbing. "Oh, Corse, Corse," she said brokenly. "Why did it have to happen?"

What had she called him? Corse? Was that his name?

The air smelled strongly of whiskey and burning coal oil from the smoky lanterns. He wanted desperately to ask her who she was, a complete stranger, to display such grief.

A handsome man with a waxed mustache moved forward and caught her by the arm. A diamond ring caught the faint light for a dazzling second.

"Come, Miss Dempster," he said smoothly. "Save your tears for the funeral tomorrow." Then, in a lower tone he said, "A damned good show, Etta."

"I had to rub my eyes to bring tears. Corse's face . . . my God, I hardly recognized him, Marcus."

"Fists and boots of the men who jumped him, I'm afraid, Miss Dempster." The man's voice was normal now for there was more shuffling of feet, new faces coming to the edge of the coffin to peer down at its occupant.

The man in the casket was bewildered, as much as his ravaged mind would allow. Why was he here? And who was he? Corse Betain, someone had called him. But when he tried to think who he might possibly be other than Betain, he couldn't remember. His mind seemed dark and empty of the past.

"Oh, our estimable undertaker," Marcus Telfont said lightly. "Let me give you a hand with that coffin lid, Wilbur. I think we've had him on display long enough."

The man in the casket cried desperately to keep them from sliding the coffin lid into place, but there was no sound from his throat. His vocal chords as well as the rest of him seemed dead. Only his brain was alive and that only minutely.

There was a scraping of wood, then the coffin lid slid into place. Light and sound, the faces, everything was suddenly blotted from sight. And he lay in darkness, save for a faint light that seeped in through the cracks, where the sides of the coffin were not expertly joined to the bottom.

This, then, was death. . . .

Lassiter was one of the last to have a glimpse of the man in the coffin. He happened to be standing next to a man who had come with a lantern. And before the coffin lid was lifted into place, he saw the face, lumpy and swollen from deep cuts and abrasions. The purplish eyes seemed sealed shut.

But in that moment he saw something that almost made him cry out. At the hairline, where the skin was reasonably untouched by violence, the lantern light flickered briefly on moisture—beads of sweat so miniscule as to be almost invisible.

The man in the casket was perspiring.

Wilbur Dover, the undertaker, drew a long screwdriver and four brass screws from his pocket. "I'll just fasten down the lid," he said in his small man's squeaky voice. He had the face and eyes of a predatory fox. "Etta Dempster's the only one who'll grieve, likely, an' she don't want the coffin opened at the funeral."

While Lassiter watched with a dry mouth, Dover quickly secured the lid.

Lassiter stepped back, one hand on his gun. He eyed the two dozen men and women in the barn. Etta Dempster, narrow-waisted in a black coat, was being led away by Marcus Telfont. Telfont's posture suggested the army. The girl's head was bowed as if she might still be sobbing. But Lassiter couldn't be sure because of the babble of voices.

"Wa'al, good thing he's dead," a man was saying. "They'd have got him one way or another."

"Was he to come back from the dead," a gaunt man chuckled, "he wouldn't last no longer'n a fly on a hot stove lid."

"Lemme give you a hand," Lassiter said, and before anyone could protest, took one corner of the coffin. He helped three other men carry it out to Wilbur Dover's light spring wagon and slide it into the bed.

Lassiter rode behind the wagon, counting off the passing minutes in his head, wondering just how long a man in a coffin could last with a limited supply of oxygen. One thing to be thankful for—whoever had constructed the crude coffin had not joined it too well at the corners. Would those slight gaps allow enough oxygen to reach the lungs of the man trapped inside? For trapped he was. Lassiter was sure of it. He was also sure of another fact. Dead men did not perspire.

Three men rode along behind the wagon, Lassiter following.

"You reckon it was Telfont's men who waylaid Betain?" one man ventured.

"I wouldn't go talkin' about it, was I you, Henry." The speaker nodded toward Lassiter's tall figure on the black horse, noting the ease with which he sat his saddle and the strong, aquiline features. "Who's he?"

But they knew better than to ask questions. It just wasn't done, not in the West. Nosey people had been known to end up in very sorry condition.

Lassiter groaned silently because Dover seemed to be keeping the wagon team to a crawl. If the undertaker dawdled too much, Lassiter knew, he'd have to make a move to free the man from the casket before he could possibly suffocate. He eyed the three men, calculating the odds. And there was also the possibility that Dover, singing under his breath, was armed.

Lassiter stayed back in the shadows, fretting, while the wagon and the three riders went around behind the Dover Store and headed toward a lean-to in the alley. On the lean-to was a sign: UNDERTAKER.

Dover tied the team, then used a key on the large padlock and opened the door to the lean-to. "Let's get this inside," the little man said. "Then we'll go over to Teeley's an' have some whiskey. God knows, it's somethin' to celebrate. Him bein' dead kinda makes up for all the *dinero* he got away with."

"Not quite," one of the men said sourly.

"Careful in the dark," Dover grunted. "We'll set her right here on these here sawhorses."

Lassiter saw Dover and the men emerge. Dover padlocked the door and they all walked around the building toward the saloon on the far side of the street, the three men leading their horses.

As soon as their voices faded, Lassiter went to work on the large padlock. He shook it and pulled hard, but nothing snapped. He groped in the dark, hoping to find a piece of metal he could use as a crowbar, but he found nothing.

Above the store were darkened windows, possibly living quarters. To one end of a long and wide porch was another room, also dark.

He picked up a stone, tapped on the window glass and finally made a hole big enough for his arm. With cold sweat dampening his face, rolling down his back, he reached up and unfastened the window. He slid it up. Thankfully it didn't screech. Throwing a long leg over the sill, he stepped inside. A strong odor of formaldehyde stained the air.

Enough light from the moon filtered through the window so that he could see to pick up a screwdriver from a littered shelf. Soon he had the coffin lid removed. And just in time. Betain was gasping for breath. In a bar of moonlight Lassiter could see the puffy lips move, but no sound came. Betain was a big man and it took all of Lassiter's strength to pull him out of the coffin and set him on a narrow bench. It was like trying to maneuver a roll of canvas. Betain toppled to the floor where he lay with arms outflung, eyes open in the ravaged face. They were bright with fear.

"I don't know what it's all about, Betain," Lassiter panted, "but I bought into this game so it looks like I'm stuck."

Lassiter searched for something to use as weight for the coffin, and found three kegs of nails near a stack of boards. These he placed in the coffin and packed gunnysacks around them so they wouldn't roll.

Not quite Betain's weight, perhaps, but close enough.

When he had replaced the screws and tightened the coffin lid, Lassiter leaned down. "Can you walk?" he whispered.

"Walk where?" Betain said, speaking so low that Lassiter could barely hear him. He had to bend closer to the lacerated lips as Betain added bitterly, "This time they'll probably finish the job."

"Who'll finish the job?"

Lassiter repeated the question, but all Betain said was, "I don't know."

"Seems you don't remember much of anything."

"Everything's blank. As if a curtain had come down."

"Do you have any friends here?"

This time Betain seemed about to laugh but stretching his lips proved too painful. He winced. "I doubt if I do," was his almost unintelligible reply.

Lassiter cocked his head, listening to the distant laughter coming from Teeley's Saloon. It had taken him the good part of twenty minutes to get Betain out of the coffin, substitute the nail kegs and reseal it. At any time Dover might return with friends.

Hardly had the thought crossed Lassiter's mind than he heard footsteps approaching and the murmur of voices. He straightened up, his mouth hardening into a grim line.

As a key rattled in the padlock, Lassiter hauled Betain to his feet and walked him, stumbling, to the far end of the long room and behind a pile of coffins stacked almost to the ceiling.

The lock clicked. Dover staggered in, followed by two other men. Dover lit a lamp on the shelf. As pale yellow light washed over the room Lassiter recognized Marcus Telfont, tall and ramrod straight, the waxed mustache halving a haughty face.

Telfont pointed at the casket on the sawhorses. "I want to be sure Betain's in there."

"So that's why you hurried me away from my whiskey. Hell, Marcus, dead men ain't been known to walk around. That right, Joe?"

This was addressed to a man slightly over six feet tall with a surprising spread of shoulders and a brutal face.

"Let's open it up," Telfont snapped.

Joe Gilbey groaned in annoyance. He got hold of one end of the coffin, lifted it a few inches and let it fall back on the sawhorse with such force that it shook the floor.

"He's in there, all right," Gilbey said. "Heavy as hell he is. Why go to all that bother just for a look?"

"While I was drinking at Teeley's I got to thinking about something is all," Telfont was saying. He was debonair, the kind of man who would appeal to women, a man who could be gracious or deadly if crossed. "It didn't strike me as significant at the time. Only later."

Dover opened a drawer and came up with a bottle. "What the devil are you talkin' about, Marcus?"

"Moisture at the hairline."

"Your imagination," Dover said, passing the bottle.

"Tell me, is it possible for a dead man to sweat?"

Dover gave a short laugh, took the bottle from Gilbey and passed it to Telfont, who shook his head. "Never did see a corpse that sweat. No siree." Dover laughed again.

"I swear, the more I think about it the more I'm positive Betain was sweating."

"Oh, hell, that's impossible, Marcus. I was right there an' didn't see it."

"It was at the last, just before you covered him with the coffin lid."

Dover sighed. "Well, if you insist." He picked up a screwdriver.

"On the other hand," Telfont said, staring thoughtfully at the coffin, "if there did happen to be a flicker of life, it's gone now."

"How so?"

"He's been without air for well over half an hour,"

Telfont said with a hard smile. "Besides, I've got things to do." He glanced at the heavy gold watch he removed from his broadcloth vest.

"And her name is Dempster," Joe Gilbey said with a grin.

"Never mind that, Joe. Although with Betain out of the way, I certainly will have more freedom of movement than before." Telfont was stepping to the door when he happened to glance to his right. "Who put a hole in your window?" he asked Dover sharply.

Dover looked across the room in surprise. "Be damned," he muttered. "When'd that happen?"

Lassiter, at the far end of the room, his body propping up a sagging Betain, drew his gun.

"I . . . I can't stand up any longer," Betain whispered. "My legs are going. . . ." This spoken in a voice louder than intended.

Telfont whirled, saying hoarsely, "What in the hell was that?"

As Telfont started to reach under his coat for a weapon, Lassiter stepped into view. Telfont froze. Gilbey, at the door, spun around and saw lantern-light running down the blue steel barrel of the .44 clenched in Lassiter's hand.

CHAPTER THREE

Telfont quickly regained his composure, his right hand dropping to his side. "You helped with the coffin, I remember. Who are you?"

Instead of answering, Lassiter gestured at Dover with the .44. "Get their guns. Quick. I won't tell you again!"

Dover's face whitened. "Just a minute there," Telfont said to Lassiter in a tough voice.

"*Do it, Dover!*" Lassiter roared.

Dover had lifted the lamp, intending to take a closer look at the broken window. His hand trembled as he set it down.

"Turn your backs," Lassiter snapped at Telfont and Gilbey. His only chance to get a wobbly Betain out of the building, Lassiter knew, was to bluff it. And then they had to get out of a town where, from all he could gather, most of the residents seemed pleased by Betain's "demise." What would happen to Betain when it was learned he was alive was anybody's guess.

"You can't order me around," Telfont said stiffly.

"Can't I?" Lassiter asked softly, his defiance punctuated by the metallic sound of his .44 coming to full cock as he pulled back the hammer. In the stillness, the three men holding their breath seemed impressed.

Muttering, Telfont did as ordered. He gave Gilbey a nod to do likewise. When their backs were turned, Dover crept toward them, looking back over his shoulder at Lassiter.

"I gotta do like he says," Dover whined as he reached around Telfont and got his gun from under the dark coat. It was a .45 with polished cedar gungrips.

"Put it on the floor," Lassiter snapped. When this was done, an ashen-faced Dover moved gingerly toward Gilbey's broad back.

An impatient Lassiter told him to hurry.

Dover's hand shot out quickly. His fingertips had just touched the butt of Gilbey's gun when there was a commotion back where the coffins were stacked. Betain had been leaning against the coffins, legs braced. Suddenly his legs gave way and he was stumbling against Lassiter. Somehow Lassiter retained his balance. Betain pivoted and fell heavily to the floor.

Telfont was looking around at Betain in amazement. "I told you he was alive," he said hoarsely.

Gilbey also had turned his head. He stood with his mouth slowly opening as he stared in fascination at the man on the floor. Betain was a sight: his swollen face covered with dried blood, clothing torn, now on his hands and knees staring up at Lassiter out of those awful eyes.

"Don't let them kill me," he begged. "Pull me up."

"Dover, do what I told you!" Lassiter snarled.

But Dover was immobilized with fear, obviously too frightened to seize Gilbey's gun as ordered. Lassiter was caught in a bind, and burdened with a man half out on his feet who was trying to lever himself up from the floor by clutching desperately at Lassiter's left arm. Pulled off balance by Betain's weight, Lassiter tried to throw him off, but Betain's fingers were gripping the sleeve of his work shirt.

As Lassiter took two stumbling steps sideways, Gilbey was given time to throw himself flat on the floor and rip his gun from its holster. Gilbey fired and missed. But Lassiter's shot whipped across the back of Gilbey's right hand. A spurt of blood, a howl of pain from Gilbey. A thunking sound as the gun torn from his hand slammed against the wall.

At the same time Telfont tried to snatch up the gun Dover had placed on the floor. But by then Lassiter was literally dragging Betain at an erratic run toward the door.

One of his shoulders rammed Telfont, who was just opening his mouth to yell. The downward sweep of Lassiter's gunbarrel to Telfont's right temple silenced the man. Telfont's knees sprang apart. He tumbled to the floor and lay still.

From somewhere above them a woman screamed. "Wilbur, Wilbur, what's goin' on down there!"

"Stay out of it!" Lassiter warned the quivering Dover. Then he was throwing the door open. The blessed night air rushed in to dissipate the gunsmoke that lay in oily layers in the lean-to. Telfont was stretched out, bleeding slightly at the temple.

Propping up Betain with one hand, Lassiter

grabbed Telfont's gun and the one knocked from Gilbey's hand. Gilbey was sitting up, cradling his bleeding hand. His face was white.

"If you ruined my hand, I'll kill you," Gilbey snarled through his pain.

From above the woman's scream had turned into a whimper. Lassiter threw the two guns out into the darkness and got hold of Betain, who had sagged against the door frame.

"Keep your mouth shut or I'll be back!" Lassiter warned Gilbey and Dover, then hurried Betain out into the darkness.

"Can you set a saddle?" Lassiter panted as he moved Betain into the thickening shadows.

"I . . . I don't know," Betain gasped.

"We'll have to ride double."

Although barely thirty seconds had elapsed since Gilbey's gunshot, there was the sound of running footsteps from the direction of the saloon.

As Lassiter boosted Betain behind the saddle of his black horse, he heard the sounds of men in the street out front. They were arguing about where the gunshot had come from.

"Downstairs," the woman screamed from above. "Bandits. Must be a dozen of 'em at least—"

"Likely just a coupla drunks," a man said loudly. "Mrs. Dover's just imagining—"

And then, despite Lassiter's warning, Wilbur Dover began to yell. "Back here, boys! A killer's loose. . . ."

By sheer strength, Lassiter held Betain upright behind the saddle. Then, with the horse already skittish because of the yelling and the unusual burden, Lassiter vaulted into the saddle. His firm hand on the reins settled the animal down.

In the faint light he could see the bulky building that housed the general store and beside it the lean-to glowing in the lamplight. Across the alley were sheds and thick cottonwoods. Windows of nearby residences were beginning to show lamplight as the occupants were roused by the commotion.

Quickly Lassiter spurred the horse into the cottonwoods and kept going. As he crossed weed-grown empty lots he half expected a rifle bullet to seek him out. But none came. With one hand on the reins, he used the other to wipe the cold sweat from his brow.

"That was a close one, Betain," he said over his shoulder. But the man didn't reply. He leaned against Lassiter, both hands locked at the waist, hanging on in desperation.

CHAPTER FOUR

Telfont staggered to his feet. His handsome face was ugly with its smear of blood, his lips twisted under a waxed mustache. "Listen to me," he hissed at Gilbey and Dover. "Not a word about Betain being alive. *Not one word!*"

They stared at him in disbelief as the first of the men swarmed into the lean-to.

Alberta Dover came clumping down the outside stairs. She was a large woman in a tight-fitting faded green wrapper that failed to hide her jiggling mounds of fat. Jamming a plump elbow into the backs of the men near the door, she moved into her husband's undertaking parlor.

This part of the business she hated, but Wilbur insisted they needed the extra money it provided. She privately felt that he rather enjoyed fixing up the corpses for display. Only this time he was being cheated because there was to be no open coffin for the funeral tomorrow of that swindler Corse Betain.

She pushed her way to her husband's side. There

was a stricken look on his face as he stared with a baffled expression at the coffin resting on two sawhorses.

"Wilbur, what happened?" she demanded.

"Nothin'," he snapped. "A gun went off. I thought I seen somethin' outside. But I never—" Telfont nodded his head slightly in approval.

The corpulent Mrs. Dover began to protest indignantly, but Telfont, wiping blood from his face with a linen handkerchief, silenced her with his cold eyes.

"I'll take care of things, Mrs. Dover," he said, an edge to his voice.

A tall, black-bearded man with a star on his vest was scowling at Telfont. "What's this all about, anyhow?" The sheriff swung his gaze to Wilbur Dover, who seemed ready to faint. "Speak up, Wilbur."

"Well, this fella, you see, he must've got in here by bustin' my window—"

Telfont interrupted him. "A man followed us over here," Telfont said, picking up his hat from the floor where it was in danger of being trampled. "He had been in a card game with Joe Gilbey. He thought Joe had cheated him. A familiar pattern, Ian. Now, I've got to get Joe over to Doc Maydon and look at his hand."

Ian McKenzie fingered his bearded jaw. "What man you talkin' about, Marcus?"

"A stranger. Don't know his name, but I will." Telfont looked at the staring faces in the wash of lamplight. "Go back to the saloon and tell Teeley that I said the whiskey's on me. I'll be over in a minute."

This was followed by a few half-hearted cheers and an exchange of glances.

"As I said, just a personal matter," Telfont said when the men had left and the skeptical sheriff remained. "I'll run into this hombre one of these days. Go join the boys, Ian." He gave the sheriff a gentle shove toward the door. McKenzie started to bristle, then his heavy shoulders shrugged. "Reckon you won't talk about it. So that's that. Good thing nobody was killed or it'd be a different matter."

When the sheriff shuffled out to join the others heading for Teeley's, Mrs. Dover said, "Wilbur, you git upstairs to bed."

Telfont shook his head. "I want a few words with your husband. He'll be along in a minute."

She grumbled but finally left. Her heavy footsteps thumped on the outside stairway.

Telfont closed the door and gripped one of Dover's thin arms. "You listen to me, Wilbur. I want Betain's funeral to go on tomorrow as planned. Act as if nothing happened."

"But what about . . . Betain?"

"My hunch is that the stranger will get Betain far out of town. Corse Betain knows damn well after the beating Gilbey and friends gave him that he's no longer welcome in Sunrise."

"But how can I bury Betain when I seen him alive?"

"You saw somebody who looks slightly like him. You have to admit that you couldn't recognize that face as belonging to Corse Betain. Not the Betain we knew."

"Well, he's purty beat up an' all, but I—"

"Let me ask you something, Dover." Telfont's voice was suddenly ice. "Who owns the building where you and your wife live and earn a respectable living?"

A guarded look creased the narrow face. "Well . . .

you own it. Since you bought it from Corse Betain—"

"And that means I want you to forget all about seeing Betain. The man you saw was an impostor. The funeral is tomorrow . . . as planned."

"What you mean is I got to do what you ask—"

"If you don't, I'll see you and your wife out in the street. One way or another."

Dover's shoulders suddenly collapsed in his slightly-built frame. "I . . . I'll do what you want, Marcus."

Telfont slapped him on the shoulder. His head pained him but he managed a dazzling smile for the little man's benefit. "I always knew you were a man of reason, Wilbur."

Telfont and Gilbey stepped out into the shadows. As they walked toward Doc Maydon's house, Telfont gave Gilbey his orders. "Joe, you take two—no, make it three men with you. You're one of the best trackers in these parts. You run down Betain and his friend." Telfont spoke through his teeth. "I don't want either one of 'em to come back here. Ever!"

"You mean finish 'em off."

"Hide their bodies. Maybe in a cave. There's plenty around here."

Telfont accompanied Gilbey to the doctor's quarters. Doc Maydon, thin and gray-bearded, asked no questions as he dressed Gilbey's injured hand. Then the doctor looked at the faint gash at Telfont's temple. "Want me to take care of that?" he asked without much enthusiasm.

"I stumbled into a door. I'll have it taken care of."

When they were outside again, a startlingly white bandage on Gilbey's right hand, Telfont said, "Get three of our men and be on your way. A good tracker like you should have the job done by daylight."

"That stranger ain't gonna die easy," Gilbey snarled through his pain. "For what he done to my hand."

Telfont rode to the Dempster house. There was no one left in the yard and the big double doors of the barn were closed. A starched servant named Fiano Blank let him into the house and quickly departed.

Etta Dempster, wearing a black dress, came slowly down the polished stairs from the upper floor. "Well . . . quite an evening."

He lifted his hat and sailed it onto a sofa. "Yeah, quite."

"What happened to your head?" She came closer, enveloping him in a cloud of perfume, to inspect the wound with soft fingers. He winced.

"I bumped into a wall."

She stared at him out of black eyes. When she moved, her skirts rustled. "I heard shooting in the distance. Trouble?"

He shook his head. She washed his wound with hot soapy water in the kitchen and then applied arnica.

"I see you're wearing mourner's black," he said, referring to the dress that fit every voluptuous curve. Her father had left her the big house and the ranch, but he hadn't left her any business sense.

"Glad you won't have to marry Corse Betain?" Telfont asked her when they were sitting in the parlor. Fianca, the maid, had been dismissed for the night.

"It depends," she said and gave him a mysterious smile.

He looked at her sharply. "A change of heart?" The clock on the mantel ticked the subtle passing of the seconds. "I thought you were sick of his gambling—"

"Among other things," she said sweetly. "I'm wondering if you didn't bring in those two card sharps to trim him."

It wasn't easy for Telfont to manage a straight face, what with the pain in his head and the direct way Etta was looking at him, that half smile still curving her full lips. "Why would you say a thing like that?" he demanded finally.

"Oh, I've heard talk. Others have said it too."

"I'm the one who warned Betain to stay away from them."

"Knowing all the time that to tell him to do something would mean he'd do just the opposite. A man dedicated to having his own way." She sighed and he watched the stirring of her breasts under the tight bodice. This she noted and her smile deepened. "No, to tell the truth, I'm relieved that I won't be Mrs. Corse Betain. Only . . ." She let it dangle.

"Only what?" he asked sharply. He did not like it when she played games.

She turned toward him on the sofa, knees together, and looked at him earnestly. "Only there was a sum of money coming to him."

"How do you know that?" Telfont demanded.

"He wrote his father, asking that their quarrel be patched up."

"Quarrel?"

"What it was I have no idea. It was the first I'd heard of it. Anyway, Corse wrote to his father at a ranch somewhere in New Mexico, I believe it was. Telling the old man about plans to bring a railroad into the valley and saying he needed money."

"So?"

"His father finally answered. Said he was selling a herd of cattle and would be bringing the money in gold."

"Why didn't you tell me this before?"

"Because I thought I was going to marry Corse."

"And now that he's . . . dead . . . you turn to me?"

"Precisely." Her black eyes were candid.

"Tell me more about this money," Telfont urged, his temper cooling.

"Nothing much more, only that his father wrote that on his trip north he'd be accompanied by someone named Lassiter."

"Lassiter!" Through Telfont's mind spun things he had heard about the man. Some said he was a known killer, others called him a benefactor. Then his mind locked onto the image of the dark face of the stranger who had ridden away with Betain.

"You seem suddenly thoughtful, Marcus. I only mentioned the money because Corse was so sure it would arrive." She plucked at the taut black silk of the dress binding her knees. "Now that Corse is dead, what will happen to the money?"

A bitter laugh escaped Telfont. "The money." Where was Betain's father? he wondered. Had Lassiter killed him and taken the money for himself? No, that didn't make sense; Lassiter would never have come to Sunrise if that had been the case. He would have kept going. But Lassiter knew about the money, of course. Maybe he had some message from the father. Maybe he was bringing the money himself, the old man stricken with an illness. But one thing was sure: Lassiter had the money to give to Corse Betain. That was why he had gotten him out of the coffin. Telfont was excited.

Then he thought of Gilbey, who by now was many miles away.

He had sent Gilbey and company after Betain and the stranger. And Gilbey had such a trained eye for sign that he could track a horse shod in wolf skin across a sheet of ice.

Betain and the stranger Lassiter were as good as dead. Gilbey would finish them as ordered. And Gilbey was keyed up more than usual because the knuckles of his right hand had been dusted by Lassiter's bullet.

Gilbey would be his own vicious self right to the end, and there was no chance of calling him back. It'd be impossible to find Gilbey and his three men in this vast mountainous country with its hundreds of deep canyons and high mesas and impossible passes. No, it was over and done with.

As was Corse Betain's wild scheme to bring a narrow gauge railroad to Sunrise Valley to serve the cattle and sheep ranchers and the silver mines in the mountains. Most residents of the valley had bought stock. Victoria Reed, for one, owner of the Plato Mine, had invested heavily so as to move silver ore over rails instead of relying on the road that washed out each spring.

But Betain, flushed with success, had the instincts of a true gambler. The urge to better his position had produced Hardesty and Rock, a well-dressed pair who drifted into town with apparently unlimited funds. Betain, in frantically trying to climb the shaky ladder of doubling his stake, came up with zero.

It turned the whole countryside against him. And it was no surprise when he was beaten, supposedly to death, by mysterious assailants behind the Dempster barn.

Etta lifted her face, her black eyes reflecting the lamplight. "Just supposing the money *did* arrive from Corse's father. With Corse dead, I need a strong man. Why couldn't we share it?"

"Perhaps." No use telling her the truth, that the secret of the money would probably die with the man known as Lassiter. "One good thing about Betain being dead. We no longer have to sneak around in the dark."

"It was rather exciting, keeping out of Corse's way."

"But dangerous. He had a temper."

"That got worse, the more money he lost." Wearing an inviting smile on her full-lipped mouth, she got up with a rustle of skirts and reached for his wrist. "Why don't we celebrate?"

She led him up the staircase, her hip brushing his at each step. . . .

CHAPTER FIVE

Lassiter's black horse was tiring from the double load. Lassiter peered ahead in the darkness, hoping for some sign of a ranch. They were nearly ten miles west of Sunrise, still on the main road. Another mile or so and in the light of the three-quarter moon he saw a corral and several horses only thirty yards from the road. The small house beyond the barn was dark.

"You need a horse," Lassiter said to the man sagging behind him. "I don't have time to dicker for one. I'll try and get it back to the owner and pay him for it. That's where you come in."

"Me pay for it?" Betain gave a squeak of laughter. "My pockets are empty. Not even one red cent."

"You'll have money, in time," Lassiter said mysteriously.

"Tell me how."

"Never mind for now. Can you stay on this horse till I get back?"

"Do my damndest. And . . . and thanks, mister. I don't know your name but I'm sure obliged to you."

"The name's Lassiter." He watched the swollen face for a reaction, wondering if old Xavier had mentioned him in a letter.

"Lassiter," Betain mused, sounding as if every part of him was hurting. "First name or last?"

"Just Lassiter."

"Come back for me," Betain said hoarsely when Lassiter helped him back from the horse to the saddle. "I . . . I'll never make it on my own."

Lassiter nodded, and took up his catch rope. He ducked through a rail fence and trotted toward the corral, every nerve stretched to the screaming point. When he reached the corral, the three horses penned there began to mill and snort.

"Quiet, you bastards," he hissed and shook out a loop.

He finally had a brown horse snubbed to the corral fence. Lassiter eyed it. The horse wasn't much. But neither were the other two, he realized upon closer inspection. And he couldn't delay while trying to find another ranch. Next time he might not be so lucky.

In the adjoining barn he groped in the dark until he located a saddle and bridle.

As he threw the saddle onto the back of the fidgety brown horse, he heard a low growl. Lassiter stiffened. A large dog with a graying muzzle stood a few feet away, legs braced.

"Easy boy," Lassiter whispered, "easy."

Watching the growling dog out of one eye, Lassiter kneed the horse and got it to suck in its stomach so he could tighten the cinch. Then, careful not to make any sudden moves that might upset the ancient dog, he worked the bit into the horse's mouth.

As he was ready to mount, he froze at the sound of a footstep.

"What we got out there, Prince?"

It was the voice of an older man. The dog turned his head but continued his low growling. Lassiter stepped into a shadow and drew his gun.

The old man stepped into a patch of moonlight and peered at the corral. It looked as if he had donned a pair of pants in a hurry because half the tail of a nightshirt dangled over his rump.

The shrill, nervous voice of an old woman came from the house. "Art, you be careful out there."

Art didn't reply, for at that moment he had spotted the saddled horse tied to the fence. "Be good goddamned, a hoss thief," he breathed, and raised his shotgun into firing position. Its double barrels could tear off a man's head with the ease of pulling a pumpkin from a vine.

Lassiter stepped quietly behind the man and rammed a gunbarrel into his back. The man was tall, bony, partially bald with only a few wisps of gray hair.

At this move the old dog began to snarl. "Shut the dog up," Lassiter commanded.

"Or you'll kill me, I s'pose. . . ."

"No."

The man quieted the dog then craned his neck to stare at Lassiter in the shadows behind him. "What're you doin' here?"

"I want to borrow a horse."

"Steal him, you mean," said Art thinly.

Lassiter shook his head and got a hand on the shotgun. At first the man resisted slightly, but then he allowed the weapon to be taken. "Don't shoot me, mister. Take the hoss an' be damned to you."

Lassiter unloaded the shotgun. He threw the shells over the corral fence into the darkness. The shotgun he sent skating across the uneven floor of the corral.

Holstering his gun, Lassiter drew three double eagles from his pocket and shoved the sixty dollars into the moist palm of the old man's hand.

"If I'm still alive," Lassiter said grimly, "I'll be back with the horse or more money. Whichever you want."

"What if you don't stay alive?"

"Then we're both out of luck." Lassiter gave a dry laugh.

Art stood hunched, clutching the gold coins in his fist, watching Lassiter mount up. "That's ol' Brownie you got there. A good hoss, but just don't ride him too hard."

Keeping one eye on the old man, Lassiter unlatched the corral gate and rode through. On the chance there might be more men at the house, he didn't linger, but cantered across the open field and sent the brown horse sailing over the rail fence to the road. In the shelter of the cottonwoods Lassiter found Betain crumpled on the ground. The black horse was a few feet away, reins dangling. After tying both horses, Lassiter ran back to Betain.

"What in the hell happened?" he demanded.

"I found myself falling. But I managed to break my fall by grabbing the saddlehorn."

Lassiter glanced toward the ranch house where a

window now glowed with lamplight. He swore. He should have made sure the old man couldn't get his hands on that shotgun again.

"We better put as much distance as we can between us and town," Lassiter said. "You feel up to it?"

"You'll have to go slow," Betain said with a groan. "You have any trouble getting the horse?"

Lassiter helped him into the saddle, then told him about the old man. They started out, still heading toward the great shadowed barrier of mountains ahead.

Lassiter was gambling that up there somewhere he would find a town and a doctor for his injured charge.

Art Wordson excitedly dropped the three double eagles onto the table in the small kitchen so his wife could see them in the lamplight. "Looky what I got," he said triumphantly.

"Where in the world—?"

"Fella took ol' Brownie." He went into detail. "I got a hunch he'll be comin' back."

"You'll never see him again, Art," his wife sniffed.

"Somethin' about that fella makes me think I might."

His wife was huddled in a flannel nightgown that had faded over the years from rose to dull pink. She bit down on one of the coins. "Seems all right." Her breath hissed through a gap in her teeth. She dropped the coin back to the table. "I figured mebbe you got swindled again. Like you done puttin' our two thousand dollars into Betain's fool railroad."

"You ever goin' to stop yellin' about that?"

"I'll keep right on yellin' till we git our money back. Or the railroad gits built. Which ain't likely in either case, Betain bein' the thief he is."

Art Wordson didn't say anything to that. He felt fortunate to have the sixty dollars. Last week he'd tried to sell old Brownie but all he was offered was twenty dollars. Since everybody, it seemed, including the swamper at Teeley's Saloon, had invested in the railroad, the valley was stone broke.

He had just gotten back to sleep when he was awakened again by the sound of horses in the yard. Right then he remembered that he had been so excited about showing the gold coins to his wife that he had run off without retrieving the shotgun from where the stranger had slung it.

But he still had a weapon, and he slid out of bed to get it. An old Colt .45. But a shotgun was much better for him because his eyes weren't too reliable. A shotgun you didn't have to aim, just point in the general direction of the target.

"Lordy, who's out there?" his wife whispered.

"I'll find out." He tried to sound brave, but inside he was mush. Too much had happened in the valley lately. Just an hour ago a neighbor coming back from town had said that Betain had been beaten to death by unknown assailants. It was the latest episode and by far the worst. He hadn't dared mention it to his wife because with Betain dead there was no hope of ever getting their money back and she would yell and scream about his foolishness.

A fist thudded on the front door with such force that it rattled the hinges.

This was followed by a low growl from Prince.

"If that dog comes close, shoot it!" a man snarled.

Quickly Wordson unbarred the door. He shouted at the dog in a quavering voice and stood there in the doorway, .45 dangling in his hand while he faced four tough-looking men. It took him a moment to recognize Joe Gilbey, big as a mountain and mean as the bears that inhabited it.

"We trailed a hoss to your place," Gilbey stated. "Where'd they go?"

"They?" Wordson was thinking about the generous stranger and wondering just how much he should reveal. While he was trying to make up his mind, Gilbey smashed a left against his jaw. Although the old man saw the blow coming, reflexes slowed by age left him wide open. His wife screamed as he crashed to the floor.

Gilbey leaned down and jerked him to his feet. "Next time I ask a question, answer it!"

Although the old man's jaw was numb from the blow, he did manage to blurt out how the stranger had "borrowed" a horse. He didn't mention the money.

"How good a hoss is it?" Gilbey demanded.

"It ain't much, to tell the truth."

Gilbey gave the other three men a triumphant grin, then turned back to Wordson. He demanded a description of the stranger.

"It's him, all right," Gilbey said when the old man had finished. "I trailed him this far but when I seen the hoss tracks from over this way I figured to find out why."

Wordson was breathing hard, scared out of his wits. His wife hovered in the bedroom doorway in her faded old nightgown. "Don't hurt him no more, please," she begged Gilbey.

"You get a good look at the second man?" Gilbey demanded of Art Wordson.

Wordson shook his head.

"Why not?"

"I was runnin' for the house. Didn't want no more trouble. I'd had enough for one night."

"And now you've had some more," Gilbey said with a nasty smile.

Wordson turned cold when he suddenly remembered the gossip brought back from town by his neighbor. A rumor that it was Gilbey and some toughs who had beat Corse Betain to death.

"If the sheriff ever asks you anything," Gilbey said, "you say the stranger stole the hoss. He never borrowed it."

"But he—" Without thinking, Wordson blurted it out about the sixty dollars. Instantly he regretted it. He stood there terrified, blood on his face where Gilbey's fist had broken the skin. He thought sure the four cutthroats would demand the money.

"Don't bring up about the sixty dollars," Gilbey instructed. Then he leered. "We hang hoss thieves around here."

"Yeah," Wordson said in a small voice.

"Remember what I told you. The hombre's a hoss thief."

As they were riding out, Gilbey turned to Jack Heald behind him on a pinto. "West along the road, the old man said. That means they're headin' for the mountains for sure. An' there's only one way through. Bridger Pass."

"A lot of trails they could take, though," Heald pointed out. He was big-armed with a deep scar on his chin.

"But he's got one old hoss that ain't fit for them rough trails. An' besides, Betain is a very sick man." He laughed.

"Too bad he didn't stay dead."

"Telfont claims we didn't do the job right or he *would* be."

"He sure as hell looked dead to me," Heald said. The other two men, Quince and Chance, agreed.

Gilbey quickened their pace, gambling the men they sought would take the pass road. From here on out he wasn't relying on his ability to read sign. He wanted to get hold of the stranger. The pain in his right hand reminded him constantly of the man. Settling the score would alleviate some of his misery. Beating the living hell out of him, then ending it with a hang rope would suffice.

CHAPTER SIX

"I can't keep on much longer," came Betain's hushed voice.

Lassiter reined in. Betain's face was ashen in the moonlight. They were on a steepening road with a creek tumbling wildly to the left. Lassiter could feel moisture from it on his face. Masses of timber, dark as a giant's beard, blackened the slopes above. Stars blinked and the moon cut a yellowish swath through dumpling clouds.

Lassiter could smell the water and the pines. They had pushed on steadily enough but progress was maddeningly slow. Several times Betain had come close to tumbling into the road, and Lassiter had had to literally push him back into the saddle.

"Can you make it to the top?" Lassiter gestured above. He could barely make out what appeared to be the crest of the grade. Either it was the crest or it could be only level for a few miles until it started climbing once again. There was no way of telling because the road above twisted out of sight.

"I . . . I'll try," Betain mumbled.

For two miles Lassiter had been leading the brown horse because Betain seemed so far gone he could concentrate only on staying in his seat, not on controlling the animal.

To try and get Betain's mind off his agony, Lassiter attempted to get him to talk as he had before.

"Sometimes a fall like you had back at that ranch will jar the memory. Is it starting to come back?"

Betain shook his head with its gargoyle face. "No."

Again Lassiter spoke of working for Betain's father. "Surely you remember Xavier Betain."

"How many times have I got to tell you I don't remember him at all."

Lassiter tried his best not to let his exasperation show on his face. He felt let down. Was Betain trying to be clever, playing the role of amnesia victim? Or was his memory loss genuine?

"But you do remember your name," Lassiter persisted.

"My name might be Jones or Smith or Abernathy. Hell, I have no idea. But you say I'm Betain. I've heard others call me Betain. So I figure it's got to be my name. But far as I'm concerned, I never heard it before in my life."

"Keep trying," Lassiter urged as they continued up the steep grade. "You even see a flicker of memory, grab it."

Everywhere around them now there was evidence of erosion, deep trenches cut across the road. In places the road was gone altogether. Their horses' hooves clattered on the stones, their mounts laboring on a road almost impassable. Muzzle foam from the brown horse carried by a stiffening breeze brushed

Lassiter's cheek. He wiped it away on the back of his hand. They couldn't keep going much farther. Betain's mount was faltering and needed rest.

It looked to be only another half mile or so to the crest of the grade. But what lay beyond he couldn't tell because of the towering walls of granite. Perhaps it was just a level stretch or more tortuous switchbacks on an ever worsening road.

"Only a little farther," Lassiter said, but Betain seemed not to hear. He rode with his head down, clinging with both hands to the saddle horn, his beaten body swaying to the movements of his weary horse.

And then Lassiter heard an alien sound. In the sudden silence, Lassiter heard it again, a muted clatter of horses. Possibly riders on the move. But it seemed unlikely this time of night. A glance at what he could see of the stars through the thickening overcast told him it was nearing midnight.

At last they had reached what appeared to be the top of the grade.

"We've got to hurry," Lassiter snapped, looking back down the grade into thick shadows. "We don't want to be skylighted here."

The moon suddenly bloomed like a yellow beacon through a rent in the overcast. Something slammed into a tree trunk on Lassiter's left. And far down the slope he saw a wink of light, heard the faint crack of a rifle.

"Come *on!*" Lassiter shouted at Betain as he hauled on the reins of the brown horse. "Dig in your heels."

But Betain did not respond and the brown horse barely moved. There was a second rifle shot and a third. On the fourth shot, Lassiter fired his Henry rifle at the last wink of light he had seen, and heard the rewarding sound of a distant howl of pain.

There was more sporadic firing but by then he had gotten Betain's horse off the road and into a thick stand of pines.

He tied Betain's horse to a stump. "Try and stay in the saddle. Don't fall."

"Where . . . where are you going?" Betain's speech was slurred.

"Trying to make it hard for whoever might be trailing us."

He had dismounted, having already spotted a half-rotted pine branch. This he ripped from the tree and trotted back up the slope to the road.

There he quickly swung the branch back and forth like an oversized broom, smoothing out all sign left by their horses. It might give them a little time. Those coming up the grade, he guessed, were Telfont's men.

After brushing out their tracks nearly back to where Betain waited, he tossed the tree limb aside and then they were on the move again, deeper into the trees, following an old game trail.

"Hang on a little longer," Lassiter hissed.

"My head is spinning like a top."

"Damn it, we've got to find a place where we can hole up."

Betain wanted to know who he thought might be after them and Lassiter said, "Likely your friend Telfont."

"No friend of mine. So far as I know, I never laid eyes on the man before tonight."

A mile or so deeper in the trees they reached a

primitive road, probably an extension of the one he had noticed some miles below that branched off from the main road, really only wheel ruts through the wilderness. Trees had been cut down to bring the road into the forest, and shadowy stumps like kneeling soldiers lined both sides. The ruts were so deep that Lassiter knew they had been made by the wheels of big wagons with heavy cargo. Ore wagons, he guessed.

When it started to rain, Lassiter put his slicker over Betain's shoulders.

Just when the brown horse was about to give out, he found a cave.

There he cut off lengths of his catch rope to use as hobbles for the horses. Then he dragged in wood and got a fire going. By then the rain was coming down in torrents and he was soaked. Betain sat with his back to the cave wall, wrapped in Lassiter's yellow slicker.

Lassiter's teeth finally stopped chattering as he was gradually warmed by the roaring fire.

There was always the chance that the trackers might come this way and if so they'd have to make a stand. Out in the cold and rain Betain wouldn't last, he well knew; and he owed it to Xavier to do the best he could for his son. He had given his word and, to Lassiter, there was nothing in the world more binding.

Lassiter studied the huddled figure on the cave floor, his back to the wall. Betain needed a doctor but where to find one in all this wild country? Return to town and run the risk of getting him killed?

To try and get him talking, Lassiter spoke of the cattle ranch the father had owned. "The brand was made up of your pa's initials. Xavier Betain. Hell man, surely you remember that much."

The wind suddenly changed and blew into the cave mouth so hard that both men were enveloped in choking clouds of smoke. Lassiter's eyes and throat burned. With his eyes clamped shut, he halfway made up his mind to tell Betain about the money his father had sent. Then just as quickly he decided against it. Because of his present condition, there was no telling just what Corse Betain's reaction to such a disclosure might be. No, he'd try to get Betain to reasonable safety and under a doctor's care until he recuperated. Then go on from there. One step at a time.

When the wind had changed again and the cave cleared of smoke, Lassiter tried to joggle Betain's mind on the subject of women. "You must have known a few. Think back and see if you can't grab at a name."

But it was no use; Betain couldn't recall a one. Then he said, "Why are you trying to help me when nobody else is?"

"I promised your father."

"A man I can't even remember. Tell me the rest of it."

"I worked for him for a spell. The ramrod he'd had for so long, fella named Red Shanley, he didn't trust, for one reason or another. I took over. A few weeks ago your Pa got a letter that seemed to tear him apart. It was from his son. I didn't even know he had one."

"You mean me?"

"His name was Corse Betain. You've got his name. And folks say you're him. So I guess you are."

"I wrote to my *father?*" A burst of strangled laughter was cut short because of the pain it caused to the stricken body.

"Don't you even remember your mother?"

Betain shook his head. "I wish to kee-ryst I could remember *something.*"

"I wonder if there's a settlement up here in the mountains," Lassiter mused. "Where there's a doctor."

"You're asking me? It might as well be the moon."

In the morning a worried Lassiter put a hand to Betain's bruised forehead; it was hot. And there was a rattling sound in the man's chest when he breathed. A doctor was needed for sure.

That rainy morning Corse Betain was even more stiffened up than before. It made Lassiter sweat to get him up into the saddle. There Betain sat, wearing Lassiter's slicker, looking bedraggled. This morning the purplish eyes, what Lassiter could see of them, seemed bright with fever and the swollen face was flushed.

The only thing to do, Lassiter knew, was to press on until they reached a mountain settlement. And at the same time avoid the men who had fired on them. Had they picked up their trail, despite Lassiter brushing out their tracks and the later hard rain?

He decided to follow the secondary road of yesterday instead of backtracking to the main one. The road eventually must lead to either a ranch or a mine. Faint, comforting patches of blue began to show through the overcast. Again he had to lead Betain's horse because the man seemed incapable of handling it on his own.

During a brief self-examination, Lassiter wondered just why he had gotten mixed up in this seemingly insoluble situation. After Xavier Betain had sold his cattle why in hell hadn't he said no thanks to the old man's offer of two thousand dollars to accompany him to the town of Sunrise. Of course in these times, two thousand dollars was a lot of money, too much for a sane man to turn down. And pity for the old man had overridden his better judgment. Xavier Betain seemed to have been driven by some black guilt concerning his son.

They came at last to columns of weathered stone jutting from a canyon floor. At their base great stands of aspen fanned out across the canyon. A herd of white-tailed antelope sprang from cover and went scampering up a long incline of shale. It reminded Lassiter that they'd had nothing to eat. Did he dare risk a shot? Even though there was no sign of their pursuers he sensed they were nearby.

He came finally to another set of wheeltracks that branched off to the north. Instinctively he felt it met the main road. He was about to turn that way when he noticed two things. A weathered sign said Plato Mine with an arrow pointing straight up the road he had been following. And on the road were faint hoofprints not quite washed out by the rain of last night. Tracks leading toward the mine and the same set later heading north, ostensibly for the main road. From what he could make out there were four horses. The men who had fired on them or someone else?

At least whoever they were seemed to no longer be at the mine.

"I've got a feeling our friends came this way." Lassiter scanned the dark trees ahead.

Betain looked at him out of puffy eyes. "They must be after you. Not me. What could I have done?"

"You were beaten almost to death," Lassiter reminded him roughly. "That must prove you did something to rile up somebody."

Another possibility skipped coldly across his mind as he thought back to the aftermath of the gunfight at the arsenic springs. The layer of dust, the sound of receding hoofbeats where the two outlaws had left their horses, someone's hasty departure. Had the third member of the outfit rounded up friends and come seeking not only the gold but Lassiter as well?

A cluster of unpainted buildings suddenly loomed around a bend in the steep road. He drew rein, staring ahead. So far as he could tell there seemed to be no one about. One of the structures was a hundred feet long with only a few windows. It looked like a warehouse. After a gap of some forty feet there was another building that looked like a bunkhouse. A screen door hung open and blew back and forth slightly in the mountain breeze. Between the two buildings were narrow tracks, parallel bands of steel that climbed up the side of the mountain to disappear into the black maw of a mine tunnel. On a siding were a dozen or so rusted ore cars.

Perched on a great hump of towering rock was a fair-sized cabin reached by a long and very steep flight of wooden steps. Gray-blue smoke spiraled from the tin chimney and flattened out under the overcast.

They moved on up the road and within sight of a barn nestled in a clump of trees. Several mules had begun to bray lustily to announce their arrival at the seemingly deserted mine. So far, there had been no sign of life. Only the spiral of smoke indicated the possible presence of another human.

Lassiter passed the reins of the brown horse to Betain. "Try and handle him yourself," he said in a low voice. Lassiter wanted both hands on the rifle he had drawn. He rode on a few feet. A crisp voice broke the stillness at his back. He froze.

"Far enough, mister! Throw down that rifle!"

The no-nonsense voice of a female, deep and to the point.

Carefully he turned in the saddle to look behind him.

Standing half-hidden by a corner of the bunk-house was a tall woman. She wore a heavy gray wool skirt and cotton trousers and muddied boots; a firm jaw and tense mouth and red-gold hair in braids. One of the braids dangled across her chest. She held a rifle. He could only see one of her eyes because of the way she was mostly hidden by the wall, but it was narrowed and hard as gray steel.

"Listen to me," he began, but she cut him off.

"Either you do what I told you or I'll shoot your friend there out of the saddle."

"You own this mine?"

"Shut up and do what I told you." Her voice had become shrill. He had the impression of a nervous trigger finger.

"All right," he said and leaned down to allow his rifle to fall into a clump of weeds and keep it out of the mud.

"Unbuckle your belt!" she called. "Let your gun rig fall!"

"Now wait a minute. Just what in the hell—"

Something whooshed near his ear and he saw a blob of smoke, heard the crack of a rifle. He toyed with the idea of sinking in the spurs and speeding along the building wall and when she stepped out to throw down on him, to hope for a lucky shot into one of her legs. But such a move would leave Betain exposed. And he couldn't be sure about the seriousness of her threat to knock Betain out of the saddle.

"Look, I've got a sick man here." He gestured at Betain who had not moved from his slumped position in the saddle, acting as if he was unaware of what was going on. "I'm trying to get him to a doctor." Anger was thinning Lassiter's voice.

But all the plea gained was a second rifle shot, this one so close it ticked the brim of his hat. He turned cold. Either she was a dead shot or had aimed for his head and missed.

He unbuckled his gunbelt and let it fall beside the rifle.

"Now step down," she ordered. "I want a look at you."

He slid to the ground and she stepped out from the wall. She was even taller than he had thought at first, with a squarish face. Her thick brows, reddish like her hair, nearly grew together above a nose that was her only delicate feature. Her mouth seemed too wide and was full-lipped.

"Just what are you doing here?" she demanded, levering a shell into the firing chamber of her rifle.

"If you'll give me a chance to explain—"

"You've got it," she snapped. "Proceed."

He told her about the men who had been following them. "I ducked them late yesterday. Betain and I spent the night in a cave—"

"Betain!" Her mouth fell open. With a long-legged stride she came to stand beside the weary brown horse and peer up at Betain, saw the brutalized face, the torn clothing under the slicker. "I didn't recognize you, Corse." Her voice was icy. "You look like your face was run over by an ore wagon."

"He was beaten," Lassiter supplied. "They thought he was dead."

She still stood staring up at Betain who seemed unaware of her presence. "Of all places, I never thought you'd come here, Mr. Betain."

At first it had been informal, she had called him Corse. But now it was formal and the words cut like cold stones. Then she shuddered and looked at Lassiter. "Joe Gilbey and some men were here last night. They wanted to know if anybody had been here and I said no."

"They took your word?"

"I had my rifle to back me up. And I stayed in the house. They couldn't get in there."

He looked up at the house on the tall flat rock. Apparently the only access was by the flight of wooden stairs; either that or climb the sides of a slippery granite mound.

"So it's Gilbey," he said through his teeth.

"They left just as it was getting dark. I guess they went on up to the Point." She inspected one of Betain's hands, seeing the patches of missing skin, the swelling. She was tugging at his hand to rouse him. "Don't you know me?" she asked tensely.

"His memory's gone." Lassiter helped Betain out of the saddle, but at the last moment Betain's knees gave way and he knelt in the mud. Lassiter pulled him up. "Is there a doctor around here?"

"Up at Shelby's Point." She gestured northward with the rifle, toward a barrier of ragged peaks nearly obscured by lowering clouds.

"I'll go fetch the doctor. Can Betain stay here?"

"I'm sure he'd rather not stay under *my* roof."

Lassiter's blue eyes lashed her face. She flushed and looked away. "He's got no choice," Lassiter stated flatly.

"No, I suppose he hasn't. Who are you?"

He told her quickly about Betain's father, but didn't mention the money. "The old man drank poisoned water. I buried him."

"Pick up your guns," she said with a shake of her head. She swept the loose braid back over a shoulder. "I'll help you get him up the stairs."

It wasn't easy to maneuver Betain up the steep flight of steps, even with the two of them pushing and pulling.

Lassiter got Betain, stumbling, to a long leather sofa in front of a large stone fireplace. The warmth from the blazing logs was welcome. He turned to the girl.

"I've got a hunch you and Betain meant something to each other at one time."

"Yes," she said coldly. "At one time."

CHAPTER SEVEN

A fat woman with dyed red hair served Gilbey and friends breakfast at the only cafe in Shelby's Point. There wasn't much to the town that had once been an outlaw hideout. But then the mines had opened up. They were closed now since the bad washouts on the main road this spring. No ore could be shipped out.

It was long past dark when they had ridden in last night, tired and disgruntled. Especially so when they had found no sign of their quarry. There had been no strangers in town that day, the saloonman husband of the fat woman confided.

Gilbey was sure the stranger had been trying to get Betain to a doctor. Betain was in bad shape, Gilbey knew full well, having taken part in the damage himself. The stranger would be out of luck because, Gilbey learned, the doctor had left town. At least that was one thing that wouldn't work out for that dark-skinned son-of-a-bitching bastard, Gilbey thought. His right hand began to ache again.

He had to eat with his left hand which was awk-ward and made him swear at every other bite. Last night they had stayed in a hotel. Gilbey had paid for the room with money Telfont had given him. He had claimed the luxury of the bed because of his wound; the other three had bunked on the floor.

Jack Heald, big-armed and with a deep scar at the point of his chin not covered by his bushy beard, of-fered an opinion. "I got me a strong hunch Betain never made it this far."

"Been thinkin' the same thing," Gilbey snarled. "They was travelin' almighty slow an' might've holed up somewheres. . . ."

"My hunch is they stayed at the Plato."

"But we was there," Gilbey pointed out gruffly.

"We never really looked around," Heald said, chewing.

"I did." Hank Chance glowered down the counter. "There wasn't no brown hoss in with them mules. I wanted so bad to get my hands on that there stranger. . . ." He moved his left arm and winced. His left shoulder was padded on the top by a folded bandanna where a lucky rifle shot last evening had ripped the flesh. "It was the stranger done the shootin'. Hell, Betain couldn't hold a rifle in them beat up hands of his."

Sam Quince agreed. "Lucky shot it was."

"Lucky or not, I'm a-hurtin'," Chance complained.

"We never did look in the house," Gilbey said thoughtfully.

"How could we git in there without that Reed gal shootin' off our britches?" Quince said.

"When I was prowlin' around lookin' for hosses,"

Chance muttered, "I recollect seein' a mighty tall ladder out back of the barn."

Gilbey gave a fierce grin. "If them two ain't there, then we'll make that Reed gal talk. It's the only mine close by an' I'll bet my stake against a hole in the ground that she put 'em up for the night."

Jack Heald rubbed his large hands together and laughed. "Used to see that Victoria Reed down in Sunrise. An' I'd say, now there's a prize filly if I ever seen one."

"She can tell us what she knows," Gilbey said in a hard voice. "An' if she gets hurt in the bargain. . . ." He let it hang there. "Who'd ever know? Her livin' way up there all alone."

Gilbey was thinking of the bonus Marcus Telfont had promised him for getting rid of both Betain and the stranger.

They hurried through the rest of their breakfast and then started back for the Plato Mine.

Lassiter fingered a small notch in his hat brim. "Your bullet came pretty close," he said to the girl. "A few inches more and you'd have had my brains instead of my hat."

She smiled and shrugged. She had donned a big checked apron and was cooking them breakfast.

Lassiter pulled off Betain's boots and looked at the man slumped on the big sofa. "Do you know where you are?"

Betain looked around the room with its leather chairs, some straight-backs, and a big table. "No idea," he said.

Lassiter repeated the girl's name. "Victoria Reed.

Doesn't that mean anything to you?" But Betain only shook his head and closed his eyes.

Even the aroma of bacon frying in a big skillet with eggs and potatoes didn't rouse him.

"His memory's completely gone," Lassiter said with a sigh.

"I'm sure it is," she said as she scooped food onto two platters. "Otherwise he'd remember . . ." She bit her lip but didn't explain just what Betain might have remembered.

Betain only picked at his food and then gave up. He couldn't even handle hot coffee.

While he ate, Lassiter got the girl's history. She had been living with an aunt and uncle at the mine, as she was an orphan. Her uncle had died two years before. The previous winter her aunt had been killed in a landslide. "She was a tough woman and she defied the mountains. But they finally did her in."

"I'm sorry. And now it looks as if the mine's closed down."

"So you noticed," she said with a wry smile. She was sitting across from him at the table. "We've had washouts, too many of them this year. And the promise of a railroad didn't materialize. . . ." Her voice turned bitter as she glanced at Betain, who had returned to the sofa. Then she blew out her breath and said, "So Joe Gilbey is after you two."

"I think somebody named Telfont put him up to it."

"The mighty Marcus Telfont." Her lips twisted. "Only been in this part of the country less than a year, but he's done mighty well. Oh, yes, mighty well."

She didn't seem to want to talk any more about

Telfont. When he tried to help with the dishes, she said, "You'd better get started for the Point if you want to get the doctor. I think your friend Betain is in bad shape."

He noticed she said "your friend"—not her friend. "Will you be all right if I go?"

"I'm used to being alone."

"But this time you won't be. You'll have . . . him." He nodded at Betain who seemed sound asleep.

"Oh yes, I have Corse Betain." Her lips curled in a grim smile and she cast her eyes to the timbered ceiling.

"You seem to think it's funny," he pointed out.

"If you only knew."

"Tell me."

"It's over and done, Mister . . . What do I call you?"

He told her, then asked, "Why would anyone want Betain beaten half to death?"

"Telfont has his ear to the ground and knows what the valley residents want, is the way I'd figure it," she said sharply. "Betain is generally hated and I suppose Telfont did what he thought most people wanted."

"Hated? Why?"

"Because he embezzled funds raised for a narrow gauge railroad."

"So that's it."

"The Sunrise Valley Narrow Gauge." She gave a brittle laugh. "It was supposed to benefit Shelby's Point and the mines up here. Haul ore down to the smelter at Dancy. Also for shipping valley cattle. But it turned out to be a bad dream." She looked scornfully at the man stretched out on the sofa.

Lassiter was staring, trying to gauge the depth of

the relationship that must have existed at one time between Victoria Reed and Corse Betain, when he heard a muffled voice from the yard below.

"Two hosses, by gad. Means they're here. Bet on it!"

Lassiter sprang up, reaching for his rifle. From the front window he recognized Joe Gilbey's heavy figure standing thirty feet below in the yard. The bandage on his right hand was badly stained. With him were three men equally as large and tough looking.

Victoria came to stand beside Lassiter at the window. "I'll tell them to get out." With her rifle, she started for the door.

Lassiter blocked her. A flare of anger touched her gray eyes.

"You might get yourself shot," he pointed out. But she reached for the door knob.

"This is my property and they've got no right to trespass." She turned and looked up into his face, adding bitterly, "And as for me getting shot, I doubt it. They'd keep me alive." In her eyes was a worldly acknowledgment of the ways of men such as those in the yard.

"Come outta the house!" Gilbey shouted. "That means *everybody!*"

For an answer, Lassiter flung up one of the front windows. A man was coming up the stairs two at a time, almost silently because he had removed his boots. A bullet slammed through the open window, causing a curtain to twitch before the bullet was buried in the wall.

"Get him, Jack!" came Gilbey's shout.

The man on the stairs had a bushy brown beard and a pair of fierce eyes. Lunging up another two steps, he was almost at the window. Just then Victoria rushed for the window but Lassiter drove his shoulder into her side, knocking her to the floor. As she screamed in anger, Jack Heald thumbed a shot. Aimed at Lassiter, it came dangerously close to Victoria. All that saved her was Lassiter's thumbed shot that spoiled Heald's aim. Heald reached the narrow porch.

As Heald leveled his gun for another shot, Lassiter fired. Heald's shot went through the overhang above the porch while Lassiter's struck its moving target in the right thigh. The impact knocked Heald reeling to the edge of the porch where he lost his balance and plunged backward. He turned over once, struck an outcropping, then, yelling, disappeared from view.

Meanwhile, Gilbey was peppering the front of the house with rifle bullets, but he gave ground when Lassiter concentrated his fire. Then Gilbey was running for the shelter of the bunkhouse with Lassiter trying to pick him off. Gilbey was at a zig-zag run and made it to safety.

Then just a slice of Gilbey's face appeared at the corner of the wall. Lassiter saw the bandaged hand clutching a rifle. Before Gilbey could fire, Lassiter squeezed off. His bullet sent wood chips flying from the corner of the wall.

"They're trying to get in the back!" Victoria cried as she picked herself up from the floor.

At the same moment Lassiter heard the scrape of a ladder against the rear wall of the house. It would have to be a tall ladder, he reasoned, as he sprinted toward the back of the house. And it proved to be. Lassiter slid up an unlocked bedroom window and stared down into a lean, vicious face. Blood from an injured shoulder had darkened the man's green silk shirt.

He was swiftly climbing the ladder, his weight making it shake dangerously at each step.

He was almost at the window. Lassiter shoved a gun in his face. "Far enough!" he yelled.

But at that instant Victoria came running into the bedroom. As Lassiter turned his head to shout at her to keep back, a gun exploded almost in his face. He dropped to his knees below the window.

"Victoria, keep out!" Lassiter warned.

For an answer, a gun erupted at the window. Victoria fell, rolling. Lassiter whirled to the window in his fury. In the window was Hank Chance's narrow face, lips tight in a half-smile.

"Goddammit, you've killed her!" Lassiter cried.

"An' she was gonna be the prize—" The last punctuated by a bullet that tore a groove in the wooden floor where Lassiter had been but a second before.

Sweat dampened Lassiter's shirt despite the cold air that knifed through the open window. His heart thudded wildly, his throat so tight he thought that if he swallowed it would burst. In those few moments he looked at Victoria crumpled on the floor a few feet away, her back to him. In this light her hair seemed more red than gold. From where Lassiter crouched against the wall and below the window, he could no longer see Hank Chance.

But he did see the man's weapon, just the long barrel pointing directly at Victoria's gray wool shirt on a level with her shoulder blades. "Throw down your gun!" Chance shouted through the window. "Or I'll bust her back with a bullet!"

Before Chance could fire, however, Lassiter lunged, intending to get a grip on the gunbarrel, but Chance pulled it free the moment Lassiter left the sanctuary of the wall.

Lassiter clawed air instead of the gunbarrel. Reaching quickly through the window he did manage to get hold of the man's right arm. Chance got off one shot but with his arm uplifted, it went skyward. They stood swaying, Lassiter with his boots planted on the bedroom floor, the other man at the top of a tall and rickety ladder.

"I got him, Hank!" sang out a harsh voice from below. "Duck so's I can—"

But Hank Chance couldn't duck. Lassiter reached out, and twisted his right arm so sharply that man and ladder swayed back, no longer anchored against the wall. In his terror, Chance dropped his gun and clung with both hands to the top rung.

By then the man below had opened up with a rifle, and Lassiter pulled himself back into the bedroom. As the ladder teetered for a moment, then seemed to stabilize on its own away from the wall, Chance screamed and Lassiter leaned out. He fired down at a chunky man who was just lifting his rifle for another shot. The rifle went flying as Lassiter's bullet plowed into the man's chest, and he staggered backward into the thick brush at the base of the rock that supported the house.

"Help me!" Desperately Hank Chance clung to the ladder with one arm, legs dangling. The other arm was extended toward the window.

The ladder began slowly to tip backward. Coldly Lassiter watched him all the way down, saw the ladder splinter on some rocks, saw the man strike the ground, seem to bounce, then lie still.

Lassiter looked for the man who had disappeared into the brush, but didn't see him.

His concern now was for Victoria. As he sprang to her side, she sat up, shaking her head from side to side.

"You scared the hell out of me," said Lassiter tensely, crouching beside her.

She gave him a wan smile. "I threw myself down so hard I hit my head."

Lassiter pushed aside some of her rich hair, soft as silk against his fingers. He examined the faint bruise at her temple.

"You'll be all right," he said in relief.

Her large eyes studied him. "Is it over? Are they gone?"

"In one way or another they will be." Quickly he reloaded, then ran to the front door.

"Don't go outside!" Victoria cried, but by then he was gone.

By the time he reached the bottom of the stairs, he heard the sounds of a horse moving away from the mine at a hard run. He had just a glimpse of Gilbey far beyond the bunkhouse, bent over the back of a gray horse. He vanished into the trees. Lassiter let him go.

He searched for the others. The man with the bushy beard had expired not only from a gunshot wound but from the fall from the high porch. He found the other two behind the house. One of them lay in the brush, both hands pressed to a bloodied chest, also dead. So was the one who had fallen off the ladder. He lay with a piece of the splintered ladder thrust into his stomach. His head was twisted queerly—he had obviously been spared some pain, dying instantly of a broken neck.

Although he didn't feel like doing it, Lassiter dug a single grave out beyond the barn while Victoria stood guard with her rifle. The whole vicious gunfight had taken no more than five minutes, but it had cost the lives of three men. Although Lassiter felt no compassion for the men who would have murdered him and probably done worse to Victoria, he was sorry for the waste of human life—the pair down at the poisoned springs and these today.

When it was over, Victoria got a bottle of whiskey from the cache left over from her late uncle. The whiskey was good; it warmed and drove out some of Lassiter's bitterness.

Victoria looked drawn from the ordeal. Apparently Betain had slept through the whole violent business—or had pretended to.

"I think he was aware of what was happening," Victoria said. "How could he not hear? All that shooting and yelling. . . ."

Lassiter wasted most of the morning in making the round trip up to Shelby's Point. The doctor he sought had left the mountains, he was told.

"Probably gone to Denver," a plump woman with dyed red hair explained. "Since the mines been closed there wasn't much for him to do."

All the time, coming from the mine and returning, he had one eye open for Joe Gilbey. But there was no sign of the man.

Back at the mine he discussed Betain with Victoria. "I guess the only thing for me to do is to try to get the doctor at Sunrise to come up here. . . ."

"Won't be necessary," said a voice from the sofa.

Lassiter and the girl whirled in surprise as Betain sat up. He still had the lumpy, bruised features of a gargoyle, but the swelling had gone down somewhat around his eyes. They were still feverish and his face was flushed.

"Your voice is stronger," Lassiter said and walked over to have a closer look at the man.

"I feel better." Betain still slurred his words.

"Your memory coming back?"

The tip of Betain's tongue flicked along the torn lower lip. "No, the past is as blank as ever." Sunlight broke through a cloud to flood the parlor with light. "I'm still weak as a dried-out mouse," Betain said as he caught Lassiter studying him, "but I'll get stronger. When you leave here, I want to go with you."

"You heard me talk to Victoria, but you didn't hear the gunshots?"

"I . . . I heard it all. I was frightened, but I didn't seem able to move."

Lassiter caught Victoria's warm hand and drew her close. "Take a good look at her. You've seen her before?"

He shook his head. Victoria gave him a look and walked over to the window to peer out at the miles of dark green trees.

"You'll come along with us, of course," Lassiter said, joining her.

She shook her head. "I'm better off here."

"Gilbey might come back. With reinforcements."

"I can take care of myself."

"They almost made it with that ladder."

"I had forgotten about it. But that's no problem now." She looked up into his face, something unreadable in her eyes.

He noted how the sun brought out the lights of her hair, sparkled in the large gray eyes. The wool shirt tight across her breasts, the Levis almost too small. He caught himself staring. He looked away, feeling embarrassed.

"Tell me about you and Betain," he said quietly.

Carrying her rifle, Victoria stalked out to the high porch that overlooked the bunkhouse, the warehouse, and the mine tunnel with its tracks and ore cars. She seemed angry.

Lassiter joined her. But she refused to discuss any relationship she might have had with Betain.

"I think he's recognized me but won't admit it," she said in a taut voice. "But I guess I can understand that. Our parting was rather explosive."

Lassiter rolled a cigarette and lit it. A tendril of hair had fallen unnoticed across her cheek. He felt an urge to reach for its softness and tuck it behind her ear.

"I'm asking you again to come with us to Sunrise," he said, lighting the cigarette. "Although God knows what we'll run into down there. Betain needs a doctor, no matter what you think of him."

She refused. He tried to argue but she was adamant. He did decide to stay over, however, and not risk another long treacherous ride in the mountain darkness.

Victoria seemed pleased at his decision. As she tied on an apron and cooked an early supper, he eyed Betain slumped at one end of the long sofa, head lowered. Again Lassiter was tempted to dig up the money, extract his two thousand dollars, turn the rest over to Betain and be gone. But visions of Xavier's wrinkled old face with its trusting eyes floated through his consciousness. He couldn't forget the promise he had made to the dying old man. Such a promise to Lassiter was binding.

The venison steaks Victoria fried were delicious. Two days before she had tracked down a deer, she explained. She also had quail in the cooler and half a ham. She was not only attractive, she was resourceful as well, and an excellent cook. She extended the meal with hot biscuits and thick gravy.

Betain barely touched his food while Lassiter asked the girl questions about the mine. Now that ore wagons could no longer negotiate the roads, she had received a ridiculous offer for the mine from the Great West Mining Company. Other owners had received similar proposals.

"You think Telfont is behind it?" Lassiter asked as he ladled gravy over fresh biscuits.

"I have no way of knowing," she said. "And I haven't been to Sunrise for ages. Not since—" She broke off and looked hard at Betain, then resumed eating in silence.

That night Lassiter unrolled his blankets on one of the rugs on the floor. Betain had a bed on the sofa and Victoria took her own bedroom.

During the night the mules started braying. Lassiter took his rifle and slipped outside. After prowling for a quarter of an hour, he concluded that a bear or mountain lion had probably stirred up the mules—not the return of Joe Gilbey.

Victoria agreed with him when he returned to the house.

"I heard you go out," she said quietly. She stood holding her rifle and for a moment seemed embarrassed that she stood with him, only a loosely belted wrapper on over her nightdress. Then, on impulse, she stood on her toes and kissed him on the cheek. "Thanks for everything you've done," she whispered, and went back to bed.

For a long time Lassiter remembered the softness and warmth of her lips against his face. It was hard for him to get back to sleep.

In the morning he would leave for Sunrise. There he might find many things, including death.

CHAPTER EIGHT

Red Shanley watched Telfont pace the living room of his big house on the outskirts of Sunrise. Telfont's was a rather ornate dwelling by Sunrise standards, set on a rise of ground that afforded a view of the east valley with its miles of forest and formidable forested mountains. The two-story house, surrounded on three sides by towering pines, was known locally as "the mansion." It had been built some years before by Xavier Betain for his wife.

After his wife deserted him, Xavier decided the place had too many bad memories. He acquired a ranch in another territory and put the house up for sale. The eventual buyer was a man named Hines, who went through the motions on behalf of an unknown client who turned out to be Corse Betain. When the old man finally learned that his only child was not only deserting him, but had bought the family home for a pittance, he was outraged. It was no secret that father and son were about as friendly as two spitting tomcats trapped in an alley.

With money left to him by his mother, Corse Betain set out to make himself the most powerful man in town; he bought the livery stable, the building that housed Teeley's Saloon and the one occupied by the combination general store and funeral establishment.

Telfont had come into possession of the house and the other Betain property by way of a pair of card sharps.

This information Red Shanley had picked up on the sly since his arrival in Sunrise.

On this day Shanley was sunk in a leather chair in the Telfont parlor. Through the front windows he could see the business section of the town. Shanley, long in the torso but short in the legs, was over forty. He had a thatch of bright red hair and a bony face blotched from years in the desert sun. Until recently he had been foreman for Xavier Betain's XB spread down in New Mexico.

One day Xavier Betain had mentioned a letter from his son who was in deep trouble and desperately needed financial assistance. The son begged forgiveness for past mistakes.

Shanley, thinking his job was secure, was therefore surprised when the old man abruptly fired him, looking him in the eye and speaking of recent cattle losses. Shanley had thought he had covered his tracks pretty well. But that was before the old man hired a gunhand known as Lassiter.

"I'm goin' nawth to see my boy," Shanley overheard the old man tell a banker. Shanley learned that the old man had turned a bank draft from a cattle sale into double eagles.

When Xavier Betain started out in a light wagon

with Lassiter as bodyguard, Shanley knew what was in the brass bound trunk.

At first he toyed with the idea of ambushing the pair. But Lassiter's reputation as a hardcase with incredible luck deterred him.

When he finally arrived in Sunrise, he put his cards on the table for Marcus Telfont whom he had known for a spell in Socorro. He sensed they were kindred souls.

"So you actually know that Xavier Betain is on his way with money," Marcus Telfont said thoughtfully. He stood ramrod straight on the polished floor of his parlor. "It verifies what I'd already heard." He was thinking of Etta Dempster's story about Corse Betain anticipating money from his father.

But it was too late. Telfont swore softly. By now, Corse Betain and Lassiter were dead.

Hardly had the thought crossed his mind than through the front window he saw Joe Gilbey ride into town and dismount in front of Teeley's Saloon.

He dismissed Shanley with a "see you later," grabbed his hat and trotted down to the saloon. He got Gilbey by an arm, pulled him away from the bar and walked him quickly to some thick pines behind Dover's Store.

Gilbey's right hand was covered with a filthy bandage. The man seemed on edge. "What the hell's the hurry, Marcus?" he demanded when they halted and Telfont released the steely grip he had on his arm.

"What happened?" Telfont demanded, breathing hard.

"Heald got killed. Quince an' Chance run out on me."

"What about Corse Betain?"

"Him an' the stranger are still alive, so far as I know," Gilbey said grudgingly, watching Telfont from the corner of his eye. "You see, it weren't my fault at all—"

"Never mind, Joe." Telfont seemed relieved. He actually allowed the thin lips under his mustache to curve into a smile.

"I tell you, with Betain an' the stranger an' that goddammed Victoria Reed shootin' at us from the house—"

"That dark stranger is Lassiter," Telfont said through his teeth and glared eastward as if to put the blame on the mid-morning sun. Light filtered through the trees and the morning mists were beginning to rise.

"*Lassiter!*" Gilbey exclaimed. "I've heard of that hombre. But how do you know for sure?"

"Shanley. I described him and he said it's no doubt that it's Lassiter."

"So that's the bastard like to tore off my knuckles with a bullet." Gilbey scowled and cradled his bandaged right hand.

"You say Betain used a rifle. That means he's recovered from the beating you and the boys gave him. I held it against you for not making sure of the job. But now I'm glad you didn't."

"Why so?" Gilbey squinted at Telfont's handsome face.

"Money, Joe. Probably lots of it." Telfont was smiling again, rubbing the palms of his immaculate hands together. "Now Xavier Betain hasn't arrived here so far as I know. So that probably means that either Lassiter killed him or the old man was taken ill."

"I don't know what the hell you're talkin' about, Marcus."

"Later, Joe, later."

He saw that Gilbey's attention had been attracted by a pale-haired girl who had come from the rear of the Dover Store and leaned a mop against the wall to dry.

"Who's the good looker?" Gilbey asked, his eyes bright as he momentarily forgot his pain.

"Some female that Dover hired to help out in the store, so I heard."

"Wonder his wife didn't raise hell."

"She did. But for once it didn't work."

"Hey, I gotta see more of that there honey."

"Forget the girl, Joe," Telfont snapped. "We have more important things to do. Such as Lassiter and Betain."

They walked away together, but Gilbey kept turning to look back at the girl who had remained on the rear porch behind the store.

Ivy Eading, wearing a drab brown dress, her blond hair done in a knot at the back of her neck, let the morning sun warm her face for a few moments before returning to the store. It was disappointing that she hadn't seen Lassiter, her purpose in coming all those miles. She wanted to punish him in some way for bringing so much unhappiness into her young life. But somehow in this beautiful setting, the peaceful town surrounded by great mountains, the crisp air, the warm sun, Charlie Baxter's image was beginning to fade. And she was asking herself more frequently just what kind of life she would have had with Charlie, had he lived. She had begged him not to team up with Chick. But Charlie's luck at cards had gone sour and he needed other means of replenishing the larder. The first she had known about his wild ways was when he and Chick had held up a store in Calistro, not telling her about it until they were riding hell bent out of town. A clerk had been shot during the holdup.

And when Charlie had told her about old man Betain and the trunk, she had pleaded with him not to do it. She didn't want to see anyone hurt. But Charlie had given her his wise grin, winked and said, "Don't you worry none, Ivy."

But she had. And waiting tensely that day, some distance from the springs, she had heard the sound of gunfire. Even before investigating later, she had known in her heart that Charlie had ridden his last outlaw trail. Thanks to Lassiter.

After arriving in Sunrise, she got a room at the hotel and hunted for Lassiter, but didn't see him. And the few people she questioned didn't know anything about him.

Only one man knew of him. "Lassiter? Hell, ma'am, he don't never come this far nawth."

She knew differently. Her money was dangerously low and the second day after her arrival, she walked slowly past Teeley's Saloon, looking in a side window. She could sing after a fashion, but did she want to perform before a bunch of drunks?

Then she saw a short man with a narrow face and thinning hair on the loading platform beside the general store. He was signing a bill of lading for a shipment.

Gathering her courage, she went over and introduced herself, saying that she had worked for Mrs. Beauchamp down in Tucson and knew the business

of general stores and could he possibly give her a
job? She knew her effect on men and smiled prettily,
saying that expected funds from home hadn't arrived and she just had to find employment.

"I'm quick with figures and know how to be nice
to customers."

"I . . . I'm sure you do." Wilbur Dover licked his
lips, scowled, muttered, "I don't care what she
says." And then, taking a deep breath said, "Of
course I can use help. I pay eight dollars a week.
You can have the spare room and your day off is
Sunday."

Later, when Mrs. Dover clumped downstairs she
took one look at Ivy and demanded, "Who in the
world is that?"

"I hired her," Dover stated flatly.

"You *what*?"

"Poor gal needs help."

"Since when you ever give a good goddamn about
people needin' help, Wilbur Dover?" she hissed.

"Keep your voice down, Alberta, an' quit the
cussin'." The reprimand astounded her.

"Just one more fool thing you've done, Wilbur,"
she said after getting her breath. "Like givin' away
our savings to Corse Betain for his damn railroad."

"Shut up, Alberta," Dover said softly, his eyes on
Ivy who was bent over a lower shelf. In this position
her skirts climbed so that he could see a good six
inches above her ankles. He felt a surge of desire
that reddened his face.

When word got around about his new employee,
men came over for chewing tobacco they didn't
need or extra tinned goods or to buy a few yards of
calico for the missus. Dover was pleased for the

CHAPTER NINE

Victoria Reed had described Doctor Samuel Maydon's house and its location in Sunrise, so leaving
Betain slumped in the saddle in a dense growth of
pines, Lassiter started out to find it. He wanted to see
the doctor and explain before showing him Betain.

He had ridden half a block when a girl came out
of the rear of the Dover Store next door to where Betain had nearly suffocated in a coffin. She was blond
and quite pretty and very young. She walked jaun-
tily as if to stretch her legs. Suddenly she looked up
into his face and froze.

He touched the brim of his hat and started to ride
on, but she said, "*You!*"

Before he could say anything, she wheeled and
returned to the store, almost at a run.

"What the hell," he muttered. So far as he knew,
he had never seen the girl before in his life.

Doc Maydon's house was rather small with curtained windows and a long porch with two rocking

chairs. A neatly lettered sign said: S. J. MAYDON, M.D.

A bony, sharp-eyed woman answered his knock and looked at him suspiciously. What she saw was a tall, lean man with glittering blue eyes.

"What do you want?" she demanded when he asked if he could see the doctor.

Patiently he explained that he had a man who needed the doctor's attention. A man named Corse Betain.

The woman's mouth popped open. "But he's dead."

"Not quite."

A voice asked, "What is it, Ella?" And a gray-haired man wearing a vest and shirtsleeves appeared.

"He claims Corse Betain's alive."

"Well, it's possible, I suppose. In view of the fact that neither Dover nor anyone else bothered to get my professional opinion as to his physical condition." The doctor tilted back his head to stare through halfmoon spectacles at Lassiter.

"What'll folks say, Doctor," Ella Ormsby demanded, "if you treat Corse Betain?"

"I'll treat Betain or any man who needs help. Go fetch him," he said to Lassiter.

Doc Maydon's examination of Betain was lengthy. The only broken bones, however, were two ribs. "It's a wonder he's alive," the doctor said after binding up his chest. "Those ribs could have punctured a lung."

"He claims to have lost his memory," Lassiter said when the doctor had given Betain laudanum and left him in a room alone. "Is it possible?"

"Anything is possible." Doc Maydon spoke to the

woman. "I'd appreciate it, Ella, if you didn't mention the name of my patient."

"Very well," she said stiffly.

"You can go home now. I won't need you any more today."

When the woman had left, the doctor took Lassiter into the study, poured two shots of whiskey into glasses and handed one to Lassiter.

"You look as if you could use it." He waved him to a chair.

Lassiter sat on a sofa, the doctor across from him in a chair. "I figure Betain's in trouble," Lassiter said, "but I can't ask him about it because he can't remember anything. Or so he claims."

"Either a fact or a simple way of avoiding questions," the doctor said with a weary smile. Lassiter judged him to be sixty, with white hair and a heavily lined face. But the eyes were clear and compassionate. "Betain isn't very well liked."

The doctor mentioned the planned narrow gauge railroad and the funds lost to a pair of traveling poker players. "Betain was engaged to marry Victoria Reed at one time. But the next thing anybody knew he was . . . well, defying the mores, you might say, by living under the same roof with Etta Dempster."

So that was the source of Victoria's intense feelings against Betain, Lassiter thought. He sipped the whiskey. It warmed his blood, relaxed him. He spoke of the beating Betain had received.

"Disgruntled stockholders who caught him out alone," the doctor said. "That's the story, anyway."

"Do you think Telfont was behind it?"

The doctor thought about it for a moment, then

finished his whiskey. "I doubt it. Telfont is ambitious, but I think he's too clever to sanction the beating of a man nearly to death. However, I could be wrong." The doctor refilled their glasses. Shadows were creeping across the yard. It had been a long, hard ride down from the Plato Mine.

The doctor asked how Lassiter had come to know Betain. Lassiter told him most of it except for the buried money.

"So you've got some kind of business with Betain," the doctor said, crossing his legs.

"You'll know about it in time." And Lassiter almost added, *if I'm still alive, that is.*

"Under the circumstances, it might be wise for you to stay here. There's a spare room in a separate building out back. And room for your horses."

Lassiter agreed, and after eating a hearty supper at the doctor's, he went to his new quarters to get some much needed rest. Having to lead Betain's horse all the way from the mine and at the same time keep one eye open for Joe Gilbey had been tiring.

The doctor's offer to let him stay out of sight until Betain recovered appealed to him.

But he hadn't counted on the gossip relay of Sunrise. Ella Ormsby broke her word to the doctor and mentioned Betain's appearance to Fiona, Etta Dempster's housekeeper. Fiona spoke of it to her employer and the news was quickly passed to Marcus Telfont who appeared with a smile on the doctor's doorstep the following morning.

Lassiter was just casing his razor after shaving when he heard the doctor saying, "But I don't know whether he wants to see you or not, Telfont."

"I got off to a rather sorry start with the man and want to make amends."

Lassiter loosened the .44 in his holster and went into the parlor.

Telfont beamed. "Ah, there you are, Lassiter," he said over the doctor's bony shoulder.

"How'd you know I was here?"

"Shall we say a little bird?"

"Probably by the name of Ella Ormsby," the doctor said with a shake of his white head.

"I have a business proposition I'd like to talk over with you, Lassiter. Will you join me for a drink at Teeley's?"

Lassiter turned the offer over in his mind, aware of the flaws. But on the other hand, a talk with Telfont might possibly remove some of the pressure from Corse Betain. Anyhow, it was worth a try.

They walked together through the early morning chill with Telfont chatting amiably about conditions in the valley, the low cattle prices, the plight of the mountain miners due to the main road being washed out by spring floods.

"I've been over the road," Lassiter said coolly. "Joe Gilbey and three men tracked us up there. Intending to kill us."

Telfont swore. "Gilbey's inclined to take matters into his own hands—"

"Oh, I thought maybe you sent him," Lassiter said softly.

Telfont seemed affronted. "Not a chance of that, Lassiter. If Gilbey was after anyone it was probably you. For dusting his knuckles the other evening."

"Maybe."

They entered Teeley's with its dozen deal tables and long bar that ran the length of the room. The few drinkers in this early turned to see who had entered. Telfont nodded and took up a position at the far end of the bar.

"Your best bottle, Teeley," Telfont called to a beaming fat man with gimlet eyes.

Teeley came up the bar with a brown bottle and two glasses he had made sure were exceptionally clean. Still smiling, he looked Lassiter over. Lassiter met the small eyes so directly that Teeley flushed and looked away. He went back down the bar.

"That business proposition you mentioned," Lassiter reminded coldly as he drank off the whiskey and Telfont poured another.

"How well did you know Xavier Betain?" Telfont asked softly.

"*Did* I know him? That's past tense. Has something happened to the old man?"

Telfont looked at him, gave a waxy end of his mustache a twirl and said, "Maybe you know that better than anyone else." He spoke for Lassiter's ears only. Down the bar the men had gone back to their drinks. Sunlight poured through the sparkling glass of the tall windows. A swamper on a high ladder was filling copper lamps with coal oil.

Lassiter smiled thinly as he took a sip of the very good whiskey. He met Telfont's amber eyes, noted the amiable mouth under the thick mustache. In his light tan suit and checked vest, Telfont could be classed as a dandy, Lassiter thought. *Somehow this snake knows about the money Xavier was bringing.*

Faint irritation at Lassiter's silence tightened the

corners of Telfont's mouth. "You didn't reply to my conjecture concerning Xavier Betain."

"I worked a spell for the old man. I found him to be honest."

"That's not much of an answer."

"It's all you'll get."

Telfont stepped up close, his handsome face beginning to redden. "I don't care for that tone of voice."

"Mister, you don't fool me a bit. You hoped Betain was dead in his coffin. You sent Gilbey and three other men after us. It didn't work."

Lassiter started for the door, moving sideways, eyes riveted on Telfont's angry face. "You don't have to do that," Telfont snapped. "I'm not in the habit of shooting men in the back."

"But you might have an itch to try."

The few drinkers in the bar gasped and rushed to the far wall to get out of the way of the two men.

Telfont controlled his voice. "I'm trying to be friendly—"

"For your information, the railroad just might get built after all."

Lassiter had thrown it in just for the hell of it, but he saw the instant response on the faces. Even Teeley behind his bar looked hopeful. And the swamper on the ladder nearly fell off in his excitement.

"You hear what he said about the railroad!" he screeched down to the others from his high perch.

But Lassiter was gone, the twin doors swinging quietly to mark his departure.

Two blocks over was the sheriff's office and jail. He found a bearded man at the table, cleaning a rifle and pistol. The man wore a sheriff's star on his faded red vest. "What can I do for you, stranger?"

"My name's Lassiter. I just want to tell you that Corse Betain is recuperating from a bad beating. He's over at Doc Maydon's place."

"The hell . . . Betain *alive*?"

"Yeah. And I'm putting you on notice that I expect him to stay alive."

"Now just a minute—"

"I figured to keep it a secret, him being back in this town. But it seems that secrets are something most people don't keep in Sunrise. Just putting you on notice, Sheriff. I don't want anything to happen to Betain."

Ian McKenzie started to sputter, but before he could voice his indignation at being talked to that way, Lassiter was gone.

For some minutes the sheriff sat there thinking about what Lassiter had said. Then, grabbing his hat, he locked up the jail office and started for Doc Maydon's to see for himself.

CHAPTER TEN

Betain made good progress. His memory seemed to be returning slowly. About two more days, the doctor said, and the patient would be well enough to leave.

Lassiter thanked him. He went to a cafe on Broad Street called Lordine's. Lordine herself, a jolly woman, six feet tall, waited on him.

He was getting edgy, sensing doom as he had that day of the shootout at the poisoned springs. He wanted to conclude his business with Betain and leave Sunrise. One of these days he'd write Victoria Reed, care of the Plato Mine, and tell her how much he'd enjoyed meeting her, that maybe in the future they'd run into each other again.

He was walking along an alley on his way back to the doctor's when he saw a flurry of movement ahead. The same young blond woman he had seen the other day was standing at the corner of a shed, talking to someone out of sight. She seemed agitated. As Lassiter approached, that someone jerked suddenly on her arm so hard that some of the high-piled pale hair came unpinned and spilled down one side of her face. As she was pulled out of sight, Lassiter waited for her scream, which didn't come. He started for the shed at a run.

When he came around the corner he saw Joe Gilbey clutching the girl by the wrist, pulling her up close. "You high-handed bitch, I only asked you a civil question."

"And I tried to give you a civil answer." Her voice was low, but packed with emotion. Her dress fit snugly to reveal her soft shoulders, narrow back and definitive curve of hip. She was trying to claw herself free of Gilbey's grip.

"Please, please," she hissed. "Let me go!"

"Will you meet me at the Rock? Like I asked? I only wanta talk . . ."

And then Gilbey raised his eyes and saw Lassiter's dark face. He dropped the girl's wrist as if it were suddenly aflame and whipped a hand toward his gun. But it was an awkward move because he was using the left instead of the bandaged right.

Lassiter lunged, brushed the girl away from the shed wall and struck Gilbey on the point of his jaw. A strangled cry broke from Gilbey's lips as he tumbled over backward into a clump of weeds. The gun went flying. Lassiter picked it up and turned to the girl.

"Did he hurt you?"

She was rubbing her wrist, giving him a strange, startled look. "You again," she gasped.

He frowned. "What'd you mean by that?"

"Only that you . . . you saved me from . . . him."

With her face flaming, she ducked around him and fled to the Dover Store.

Puzzled at her behavior, Lassiter looked at Gilbey stretched out cold in the tall weeds. Lassiter walked away, carrying Gilbey's gun. As he was passing the livery barn, he dropped it down into a rain-filled barrel. *That'll de-fang him for awhile*, he thought with a sour laugh.

That evening a delegation of eight, led by Bert Teeley, came to Doc Maydon's house to confer with Lassiter. The doctor went out back to tell Lassiter, then invited the men into the parlor.

When Lassiter entered, the heavyset Teeley jumped to his feet. "The other day you said somethin' about mebbe the railroad gittin' built anyhow. What'd you mean?"

Lassiter looked at the eight faces, each pair of eyes intent on what he might be about to say. He hesitated. The clock on the rolltop desk ticked loudly.

Lassiter thought of Betain in bed in the other room, thought of the fifty-eight thousand the man would have in another day or so. "All I can say is that I've got a hunch about it is all," he said carefully.

But they began to talk excitedly at once, begging for more details.

"You'll have to ask Corse Betain when he's well enough . . ."

But this brought an angry response. "That thief!" Teeley snarled and the other seven men nodded in agreement.

"Give him a chance," Lassiter said, waving his hands for silence. In the lamplight the men's faces showed strain. These men had invested heavily in Betain's scheme and felt cheated. Now Lassiter was asking them to give the man a chance. Lassiter was hoping that Betain had suffered a temporary loss of judgment in letting a pair of Fancy Dans fleece him at poker—if the rumors of such a happening were true, that is.

He finally got them calmed down, asking them to wait two more days. Just two. He stressed the integrity of Betain's father, Xavier, saying surely some of it must have rubbed off on the son. He didn't mention Xavier's passing. Corse Betain himself could reveal it after Lassiter was gone.

The men headed for the door, not too happily, muttering that they'd give it another two days as Lassiter had suggested.

When they had gone, Doc Maydon gave Lassiter a wry grin. "The way you handled 'em, you should run for office."

Lassiter shook his head. "I'll be gone in a couple of days. Leaving behind good news." *At least I hope so*, he amended to himself.

Doc said, "Let's have a drink. You deserve it for all you've done for Betain. And I certainly do for spending a day with the halt, the lame and the wounded." There had been two gunfights in town that day. One at the livery barn and another in back of Teeley's.

After the drinks, Lassiter looked in on Betain. The swelling on his face had gone down and he certainly seemed brighter. "I couldn't help but overhear the business in the parlor. Thanks for sticking up for me although I still can't remember what you say I was involved in."

"Memory coming back at all?"

Betain rubbed the point of his jaw gingerly for it had not completely healed. "A little. Bits and pieces here and there."

"Two more days should do it. Then we'll conclude our business."

"Mind telling me what it is?" In the light of the bedside lamp, Betain watched him out of green eyes. Now that the swelling had gone down, Lassiter could see for the first time the color of Betain's eyes.

"You'll know soon enough," Lassiter said with a tight grin.

The next morning he was walking to get his breakfast at Lordine's, not wanting to put the doctor out, when a young woman called to him.

He turned and saw her in a red-wheeled buggy pulled by a fine black horse. Her hair, as black as the animal's coat, was pinned up stylishly. She wore a light wool coat buttoned at the throat. He remembered seeing her at the barn the night of the Betain wake. Etta Dempster.

"Will you ride with me, Mr. Lassiter?" she asked. Her full-lipped mouth was smiling and her black eyes were locked to his. "There's something I'd like to show you." She looked both ways along the street, then leaned over and said in a low voice, "About the railroad."

He climbed in, curious as to what she might be up to. She spoke of the beautiful spring day and of a dinner party she had given the evening before.

As she walked with him up the broad veranda steps of her house he was pleasantly engulfed in a wash of perfumed air. The door was opened by a thin woman in a gray uniform.

"Fiona, you may have the rest of the day off," Etta said, "to go and visit your ailing mother."

For a moment Fiona looked blank, but then she

said quickly, "Oh, yes ma'am, and thank you." She hurried out.

Etta turned to Lassiter, noticing that his hand rested on the butt of his holstered .44.

"Why the apprehension?" she asked, her head tilted back to stare at him through thick lashes.

"There's rumors that you and Telfont are . . . well, good friends. Mighty good friends."

Her face changed and she took a deep breath. "No longer. I've learned that Marcus Telfont is interested in only one thing and that is definitely Marcus Telfont."

"What did you want to see me about?"

She led the way into an ornate parlor. She sat in a ladder-backed chair facing him, knees together, he on a sofa.

"My father left me a ranch. It's been poorly operated. I need a superintendent. I'm offering you the job."

He smiled. "You don't know one thing about me, yet you offer me so much."

"There's talk about you all over town. How well you know the cattle business." She looked at him intently. "And other things."

"What other things?"

"How tough you are."

"With certain people, maybe."

She leaned forward. "I need a strong right arm. Someone to stand beside me against the world."

"That's pretty good. You should give speeches."

"Don't make fun of me, Lassiter." She hunched her shoulders, looked around the ornate room with its polished wood, the delicate lamps. "It's warm in here, don't you think?"

"I hadn't noticed . . ."

She stood up and threw off her cloak. Underneath was a black dress that seemed molded to her voluptuous body. "This is what is known as mourner's black." She ran her two white hands with their rosy nails down either side of her body. "I wore it for Corse Betain. But now I understand he's alive—"

"I was in the barn that evening. I don't remember you showing much grief when you thought he was dead."

"You're right. I didn't." Her black eyes snapped. "I put money in his railroad. Money that he foolishly gambled away. So I no longer need to wear black, now do I?" She gave him a tantalizing smile. "So as of this moment I am divesting myself of same."

Her fingers flew along the sides of the dress, deftly undoing small buttons, shrugging it off her shoulders until it fell in a pool of black silk at her feet. Despite himself, Lassiter felt a strong surge of desire as she came closer, clad only in a fitted shift and a pair of black shoes.

She held out both hands. "Will you come upstairs with me? So we can seal a bargain about the job you'll take?" One black brow lifted. "Or are you afraid of me?"

"I'm human. Beauty never makes me afraid." He stood up. "But first I want a look at every closet, every room in this big house."

"You think I have someone hidden who can do you harm?"

"Being careful is how I've lived so long." He gave her a wry grin and thought of taking over for her as ranch superintendent—at least for a while—to be around and see that Corse Betain got his railroad built.

Hand in hand they went on the inspection tour together.

He found nothing suspicious. After he made sure all the doors were locked, he went upstairs. He found her sitting in the middle of a large canopied bed. Her black shift and the shoes were scattered carelessly across an oriental rug.

At first she was an able and exciting partner but when she felt he was sufficiently aroused, she coolly laid down the terms of employment. He was to live under her roof and be subject to her whims.

"A stud it's known as," he said, meeting her eyes. "That's not very nice."

He raised up from her breasts and started to get out of bed. But she clung to his wrist with both hands. "I acted like a spoiled wench. And I've been told that I am. I'm sorry."

Although he had been on the point of leaving, he had to admit she made a fetching picture, framed in the sunlight, lying on the pink coverlet that set off her midnight hair.

"Am I forgiven, Lassiter?"

Then he set out energetically to prove that he had forgiven her—at least partially.

"We won't discuss business until—" She didn't finish for by then she was gasping and clinging to his strong shoulders.

When he had dressed and she had thrown on a calico dress, she followed him barefoot down the polished stairs, talking about her business proposition.

At the door he said with a tight smile, "I'll think it over."

"We haven't even discussed money." She leaned warmly against him then and said, "Speaking of money. Is it presumptuous of me to suppose that you just possibly brought a sizable amount to Corse Betain?"

His gaze narrowed and he thought, *so that's it*.

She leaned against the front door to prevent him from opening it. "For a time I thought I had strong men at my side. First was Corse Betain, but he turned out to be such a bastard. Then Telfont. But I've grown afraid of him." She touched his wrist with warm fingers, looking up into his face. "I feel that you are my salvation."

"We'll see." He had no intention of working for her. He had toyed with the idea briefly, but for a few brief moments she had rattled the chains she expected to lock on him.

Her black eyes exploded with anger. "Damn it, after today, how can you stand there and not give me a definite answer?"

Smiling, he caught her under the armpits, swung her away from the door, opened it and stepped outside. As he began walking back to town he could hear her yelling after him, but he didn't turn his head.

That morning Doc Maydon was beaming when he explained Betain's progress. "He knows who he is and remembers some of the past. Not all of it, but some."

Betain, fully dressed, was sitting in a chair at the head of his bed. The abrasions on his face were healing well. He climbed stiffly to his feet.

"I sure appreciate everything you've done for me, Lassiter," Betain said.

Lassiter shrugged. "You feel like taking a ride?"

"Yes. I want to get started settling things. And you can help . . ."

Betain had no money with him so Lassiter, over the doctor's protests, paid the medical bill of thirty-five dollars. Betain said he wanted the doctor paid because he knew how hard the man had struggled. "I owe you a lot, Doc," he finished.

The doctor looked at him owlishly. "How you've changed."

"A complete change. I had a bad spill from a horse a few years ago. And it did something to my head. Made me different. I think that beating brought me back to normal."

The doctor looked thoughtful. "Well, I wasn't here when you had that fall from the horse, but I . . ." He spread his hands. "If you believe it's what happened, then so do I." He clapped Betain on the arm and wished him luck.

"I'll need a lot of it, Doc."

Since losing his house to Telfont, Betain had been living in a suite at the hotel. When they heard he was dead, the management had packed up his belongings. There Betain exchanged the worn and bloodstained garments he had been wearing for a gray suit and polished boots.

They got their horses and started west out of Sunrise, Lassiter leading the way. "Where are we going?" Betain wanted to know.

"You'll see," Lassiter said.

They were seen by Allie Harms, a hostler, who happened to be hand-backing a rig into a slot in the wagon yard. He looked through a break in the board fence and saw Lassiter and Betain ride past. Harms ran all the way over to Teeley's where he had seen Telfont go earlier that morning. Telfont had asked Harms and some of the town hangers-on to report any movement Betain might make. Telfont was known to be generous and Harms hoped to earn a few silver dollars, perhaps even a gold eagle.

Ivy Eading also happened to see Lassiter and Betain riding at a leisurely pace out of town. Feverishly she dashed to her quarters at the end of the long porch behind the store and changed into riding clothes. She had started out when she remembered something. Quickly she returned to her room, rummaged in a saddlebag and got a grip on Charlie Baxter's splendid .45 with the ivory grips.

Swallowing, she put it in the pocket of her heavy jacket. Its weight pulled the jacket out of shape.

Wilbur Dover tiptoed out of the store, looked back over his shoulder and was standing there when Ivy hurried out.

She came to a halt, her face reddening. "Mr. Dover, there's something I've just got to do—"

"It's all right, Ivy." He patted her arm, leaned close. "Just wanta tell you that the missus is leavin' on the noon stage Thursday to go spend some time with her sick sister. . . ."

"Wonderful," was all Ivy could think to say in a shrill voice as she danced away from Dover's groping hands and started to run for the livery stable to get her horse.

Today she hoped to settle with Lassiter. Not kill him, as she had planned at first, but just wound him. With luck, she'd get him alone, away from the tall man with the scabs on his horrible-looking face. She pictured Lassiter lying on the ground, clutching an arm or a leg, wherever her bullet had gone. And she would explain that it was in payment for him killing Charlie Baxter. Then she might even unload Charlie's gun and leave it for him as a reminder.

Then she would return to town, get her things, and ride as fast and as far as possible before Lassiter could send the law after her.

She hurried to catch up and finally saw them far down the road, their horses at a walk. So great was her tension that she was close to tears. To end it today, at long last, for Charlie.

When she closed her eyes against the spring sunlight, she found it hard to visualize Charlie, and their time together now seemed blurred.

But no matter, avenge Charlie she must. Many miles to the south at the poisoned springs, she had made a vow that she intended to keep, one way or another. . . .

CHAPTER ELEVEN

As they rode, Betain was saying, "I remember bits and pieces of what you told me. But I pretended to be completely out of it because I was in such pain."

"I figured it as a possibility."

"You said my father sent you. My hunch is with some money."

"Before the hour is out you'll know for sure." Lassiter's smile was tight.

"I did write what I considered to be a masterpiece of a letter to the old man. Confessing my many sins, telling him I knew now that he was right and I was wrong." Betain turned in the saddle. "He's dead, isn't he?"

Lassiter nodded and told him about the poisoned water and the ambush. "If he hadn't killed one of the bastards, I just might not be here today."

"My father was a dead shot."

"He proved it that day."

"He paid you, of course, to undertake this mission."

"When we dig up the money, I'm to take two thousand dollars."

"Dig up the money, you say." Betain nodded at the short-handled shovel strapped to Lassiter's cantle. "I wondered why you brought that. Now I know. By the way, what is the total amount?"

"Sixty thousand in double eagles."

"The old man always distrusted banks. He loved gold. I see he hadn't changed. Minus your two thousand, for services rendered," Betain went on with a short laugh, "it means I'll have fifty-eight thousand dollars."

Lassiter studied the misshapen profile. "That's right."

"Money I will use to repay the stockholders. Of course it won't be enough, but I'll work like holy hell to repay the rest of it."

"Good," Lassiter said in a flat voice.

"You don't believe me?"

"I only hope you mean what you say."

"I do."

Lassiter couldn't tell why, but he felt uneasy. He drew rein and looked back down the road but there were so many twists and turns to it that he had a clear view of only some fifty yards. He glanced to his left, seeing the tree with the slash marks he had made at its base with a pocket knife. He almost made some excuse to postpone recovery of the money to another day.

Here the pines were thick, their scent so strong it caused the nostrils to twitch. He looked up at the pines towering into the blue sky.

"Well, here we are," he said, making up his mind. He pointed at the slash marks and started to tell Betain about the second tree with slash marks, fifty yards due south in the dense pines.

But something made him look around. He was staring into the barrel of a gun. A weapon of small caliber, to be sure, but as lethal as a .45.

Betain's healing lips were twisted in a nasty smile. "I want you to do what Victoria ordered you to do that day in the mountains. Put down your rifle. And your gun rig."

"Where'd you get your hands on the gun?"

"I stole it from Doc Maydon. Now do what I told you. Or I'll shoot you in the gut. You'll be a long time dying."

Lassiter read cold murder in Betain's slitted green eyes with their faint purplish blemishes.

Carefully he dropped his rifle, unbuckled his belt, and let it and the .44 fall to the ground.

"What do you aim to do next, Betain?"

"Why, I kill you. Then I dig up the money."

"And the stockholders don't get a dime, I imagine."

"You imagine correctly." Betain laughed and motioned with the .38 for Lassiter to dismount. When this was done, Betain carefully stepped down. The two horses, reins trailing, moved deeper into the trees.

Lassiter swallowed in a dry throat. His lips felt parched and his heart seemed loud as a war drum in his ears.

"You recognized Victoria Reed, of course," Lassiter said to keep him talking.

"That bitch. If she'd have made demands on me I intended to arrange for an accident. Owner of Plato Mine dead in premature blast of black powder. Too bad."

"I tried to take your part when so many people claimed you were a thief."

"And now I give you permission to say a prayer. Before I—"

"If your father hadn't died, what would you have done when he arrived?

"I wrote such an appealing letter I fully expected help." Betain fingered a scab on his chin. "As to what would have happened to him? Well, I can say honestly I could have put a bullet in him as easily as I am about to put one in you."

"The money isn't here."

Betain laughed. "Oh, come now, Lassiter—"

"It's buried deeper in the trees." Lassiter tilted his head in a southerly direction.

"The money is right by the slash marks. I'd let you do the digging for me, but they say you're a clever son of a bitch and you just might trick me in some way. Stand aside." Betain motioned with the gun.

Lassiter backed up, away from the holstered .44 that lay on the ground. He waited tensely, hoping Betain would come close enough so he could get a hand on him. But Betain was keeping his distance. He lowered his eyes only for a split second as he kicked the holstered revolver across the narrow clearing. And in that moment Lassiter took a forward step, but Betain jumped backward, teeth bared.

"Oblige me, if you will, by turning your back," Betain said with a cruel smile. "I find I'd rather not see your face when I shoot you. . . ."

Lassiter tilted back his head and let a sudden burst of harsh laughter roar from his throat. "You poor fool, you!" he cried as the laughter continued to pour out of him.

He saw the startled look on Betain's face, the moment of indecision. Then Lassiter flung himself to the ground. It was too far to reach his holstered .44 but not too far to grab the Henry rifle. As he struck the ground, the .38 made a spiteful roar. Bits of pine needles flung up into Lassiter's eyes. His chest struck the ground, blasting the air from his lungs. Snatching up his rifle, he cocked it and rolled onto his back. But it was too late. He saw Betain's triumphant smile as the small-caliber weapon exploded a second time. In that shattered second of time Lassiter felt as if a load of rocks had been dumped onto his left side, hammering him into the ground.

But as Betain shifted the gun for another shot, Lassiter fired the Henry. Above the roar of the gun he heard Betain's scream. The force of the bullet slamming into his right shoulder spun Betain halfway around.

At a staggering run, trailing blood, he disappeared into the trees.

Lassiter tried to get up but it was as if he were pinned to the ground.

"There he goes!" a man shouted from nearby, out of sight in the screen of trees.

"Which one is it?" Telfont yelled.

"Can't tell!" came Joe Gilbey's strident reply.

"Let's go get 'em!"

There came the sounds of men running.

Desperately, Lassiter pulled himself into the saddle and started north through the pines. There were more gunshots, more yelling, at a distance now. A man gave a horrible cry. Then silence.

Still clutching his rifle, Lassiter pushed his black horse to a fast walk, to try and minimize the sound of his hoofbeats. Fortunately they were deadened by the thick mantle of pine needles.

How many hours he stayed in the saddle he never knew and the time he traveled was a blank. His whole left side was soggy with blood, and blood had leaked down into his boot. Bright lights danced across his consciousness, interspersed with grotesque shadows. Finally he booted the rifle and found he had to cling with one hand to the saddlehorn. His head felt light as a hot air balloon, and the roaring in his head reminded him of a passing train. Each thudding blow of his heart he thought would be the last. But still he kept on.

Sheer instinct carried him to the Plato Mine. He found himself at the foot of Victoria Reed's long flight of wooden steps. He opened his mouth to cry out, but it wasn't necessary. She was already rushing to his aid.

Somehow she got him up the flight of stairs and to the sofa where Betain had lain, pretending his memory had not returned.

With a sharp knife she cut away his shirt. When she saw the wound her face blanched.

"Oh, my God," she breathed. But after sponging it with warm soapy water, the wound was not as horrible as she had at first imagined. The bullet had struck a rib and been deflected in such a way that a great chunk of flesh had been cut away.

As she dressed the wound as best she could, he took his mind off the pain by relating what had happened.

"I don't know whether Betain's alive or dead. But I feel they killed him—"

"And will blame you." She drew a deep breath. "You can bet on it." She was kneeling beside the sofa, holding the length of clean cloth she had used for bandages. "We've got to get you across the line into the next territory where Sheriff McKenzie can't lay a hand on you—"

"No." It hurt him to talk, as he looked into her gray eyes, saw their compassion, the white teeth sunk into her lower lip. "I guess I came here, sensing I could get help. But now I've got to push on. I can't let you get involved in this."

"My darling," she said with a catch in her voice, "I am already involved." She placed her soft hand against his cheek. Her eyes were shining. "I'm only glad he didn't kill you."

"Yeah, I feel the same way about that," he said wryly. She smiled, then grew serious.

"I used the last of the arnica. And the laudanum is all gone. All of it . . . wasted on Corse Betain." The last said through her teeth.

"He must've meant a lot to you at one time—I'm sorry about the way things turned out."

"I should have known better," was all she would say on the subject. Logs crackled in the fireplace, throwing the faint odor of woodsmoke into the air.

She rose from her kneeling position beside the sofa. "I'm going up to the Point. I need supplies and medicine for you."

"Wait till I can go with you," he said, coming to his elbows.

"I'll be all right. Don't worry." She placed a warm forefinger across his lips to silence him. "I'll hide your horse. If anyone should come, don't show yourself."

"Look, I don't want you to go."

"Besides, maybe I can get word of what's going on down in Sunrise."

"But you said no wagons can get through with the road washed out—"

"They bring the mail by horseback these days. And it's due."

Despite his protests she rode away, leaving him alone. The loss of blood, the long ride into the mountains had taken their toll. He reached down and felt the comforting cool metal of his rifle on the floor beside the sofa. He looked up and watched the reflection of flames from the fireplace on the timbered ceiling.

In his mind he tried to reconstruct the tragic scene outside of Sunrise. He recalled Telfont's shout and moments later the cry of a man in pain. There had been gunshots. How many? He couldn't remember.

All he knew was that somehow he had found his way to this sanctuary and been delivered into the hands of a remarkably capable young woman.

"Xavier," he said to the ceiling, "it didn't work out quite the way you planned with your son."

Then the reserve that had kept him going for so long ran out of him like water from a leaky bucket. He fell into a deep sleep, little dreaming of the bleak future that stretched ahead.

CHAPTER TWELVE

Some hours previously Telfont had stood in a thick stand of pines, holding a smoking .45 as he stared down at the crumpled body of Corse Betain. His shot had taken the man dead center in the heart.

Joe Gilbey was massaging the knuckles of his healing right hand. "You killed him, by gad. Now you'll never find the money."

"Better he killed *me?*" Telfont snarled. He was sweating.

Red Shanley brushed back a lock of fiery red hair from his sun-blotched forehead. "Well, what do we do now?"

"Find Lassiter." Telfont ground his teeth. "Put his feet in a fire and he'll tell us about the money quick enough." He looked toward the road he could see through the trees some distance away. "What in hell happened to Jud?"

Red Shanley spoke up. "Last I seen him he was ridin' hell bent for town. Leastwise that's how it looked to me."

Telfont shook his head. There was a long scratch on one cheek from where he'd crashed through a thicket after the fleeing Betain. His jacket was ripped and the front of his white shirt was blotched with sweat. "A big bastard like Jud Ream and he turns tail and runs." Telfont sounded disgusted.

"Good with his fists," Gilbey said, "but mebbe yellow when it comes to guns."

"I'd heard different," Telfont said heavily. He had hoped to end it all today, but everything had unraveled. Two days ago he had hired Jud Ream as added insurance. The big man had drifted into Sunrise with a reputation as a bare knuckle fighter preceding him. This very morning Telfont had fixed it so Ream could put on an exhibition of his prowess behind Teeley's Saloon.

Here was the proposition Telfont had made. If two good men together could beat Ream with their fists they would each get one hundred dollars. To hard-scrabble ranchers and cowhands this represented more money than they could make in two months of toil. It made them reckless so that they overlooked Ream's six feet three inches, his two hundred and fifty pounds, the broken nose, scars over the brows, and other marks left from previous encounters.

Two men, Bigg Logan and Chuck Berne, had accepted the challenge. Both were over two hundred pounds and confident of victory. A crowd gathered and bets were made, with the crowd favoring the pair of locals.

For a time Ream toyed with them, pretending to be hurt, and brought great roars from the onlookers.

Then he acted as if weary of the farce. A hammering right lifted Logan off his feet and sent him shuddering to the ground. Berne was dispatched with shattering lefts and rights to the body and an uppercut to the jaw.

Ream accepted the plaudits of the crowd; even the losers had to heap praise on his broad shoulders. It was then that Telfont took him aside and said, "Jud, there's an hombre here in town I want you to beat to his knees. Name of Lassiter . . ."

And right at that moment the hostler from the livery barn had arrived, breathless, to tell Telfont that Lassiter and Betain had left town together, heading out the west road. Telfont flipped a coin to the hostler, then with Gilbey and the other two had run to the stable for their horses.

And now, standing in the thick stand of pines three miles west of town, it looked as if Jud Ream had quit cold on them.

Telfont swore, then said, "Joe, let's find the spot where the shooting started."

It took only a few minutes. They saw the scuffed places on the ground, the blood. They found the short-handled shovel that Lassiter, half out on his feet, had torn loose from the cantle to lighten the burden of his horse as much as possible.

"We'll trail Lassiter," Telfont announced, then looked speculatively at the shovel. His gaze shifted and he saw the tree with the three fresh slashes at its base.

"The money's *here*, by God—"

He was interrupted by the sound of hoofbeats. Jud Ream came riding up, a broad grin on his scarred face. Under one thick arm he was holding the young blond who worked at Dover's Store. Her face was dead white from fear.

"She seen it all, Telfont," Ream said with a fierce grin. "She tried to git away, but I run her down. Looky what she had on her." It was a Colt .45 with ivory gun grips.

But the moment Ream set her on the ground she seemed to regain some of her composure. It took several seconds for Telfont to still the runaway thoughts cascading across his mind: bribe her, threaten her, or put a bullet into that beautiful body and bury her somewhere under the green canopy of pine trees.

Finally he composed himself so that he looked reasonably pleasant. Ream still held her by an arm, his scarred fingers almost repulsive against the delicate contours of her flesh.

"Let her go, Jud," he said mildly. "You three take turns with the shovel." He inclined his head toward the tree with the slash marks at its base. "I'll have a talk with the young lady."

Telfont looped an arm about her waist just in case she took a sudden notion to bolt. He'd had enough running for one day and didn't want anymore of it.

"Just what are you doing way out here, my dear?" he asked when they were out of sight of the three men.

"I wanted to see the country. So I took a ride." Her blue eyes were defiant.

"Yet my friend Jud Ream says you saw it all. Just what did you see?"

"Let me go. I want to get back to town."

"You keep on with that attitude and there's a slim chance you might never leave here."

It was said so softly, so pleasantly that for an instant she wasn't sure what he was saying. But when she realized the full impact of his statement, her face again began to lose color.

From deeper in the trees came the comforting sound of a shovel digging into the loose soil. Birds chattered in the trees and a flock of them, disturbed by the harsh voices of the three men, swirled into the azure sky, dark blots in the sunlight.

"I ask again, just what did you see?" Telfont persisted, a half smile riding on his mouth under the thick mustache. Today he had neglected to wax the ends and they drooped at the corners, giving him a sinister look.

"I . . . I was hiding in the trees when I saw that man with the scabbed face run away. . . ."

"Go on," he urged softly.

"He . . . he had been shot and was bleeding, and . . ."

When she hesitated, a tongue tip darting across her lips, he said, "Then what?"

"You know what happened!" It burst from her throat so loudly that Jud Ream, who had just passed the shovel to Red Shanley, turned to stare at her from cold eyes.

"I'm asking *you* what happened," Telfont said, his voice acquiring an edge.

"Oh my God, why do you keep on asking me?" Her hands were gripping the wide belt that encircled her slender waist. "You shot him, shot him dead."

Telfont shook his head slowly from side to side.

"No, you saw Lassiter shoot him dead. Do you understand? Lassiter!"

She thought about it for a minute and gradually her chin came up. He could see the delicate muscles of her throat working as she swallowed. "Lassiter?" she said, her eyes narrowing.

Telfont described him. "You've likely seen him around town."

"Oh, I know who he is, all right." Her voice was suddenly shrill.

Telfont, playing it by touch and go, pounced on this abrupt change in her attitude—from fear to outright anger. "You dislike the man. It shows in your eyes."

"He killed . . . a . . . a friend of mine."

"And you want to get even."

"It's why I came to Sunrise."

"You followed them out here today?"

"Yes."

"Thinking this might be a way to get your revenge?"

Without replying, she turned her head and stared at a granite wall north of the road a half mile or so, its face dotted with spots of green where dwarf trees had taken root.

"What sweeter revenge than to see Lassiter hang for killing your friend," Telfont said when she continued to stare at the cliff wall.

She turned then and looked at him, her eyes bright with tears. Twice she tried to speak, but faltered. Then she said, "The best possible revenge."

"Where is your horse?" he asked and she made a vague gesture down the road toward Sunrise. Telfont sent Joe Gilbey to bring it back while he and Ivy sat in the shade and talked. By the time Gilbey appeared with her horse, Telfont had learned most of her background: being taken in by Clara Beauchamp when her folks died, working in the woman's store until a wild young buck named Charlie Baxter had appeared.

Gilbey turned over the reins of the girl's red roan to Telfont. Then he massaged the scabbed knuckles of his right hand and gave her a level look. "Heard you talkin' about Lassiter. I owe him plenty. For this." He held up his hand. "An' for a punch in the jaw he gave me when I was just talkin' to you."

When Ivy refused to look at him, Gilbey snarled, "Wasn't that right? I was just talkin' to you when that bastard butted in?"

"Take another turn with the shovel, Joe," Telfont said jovially. "And cool off. Mr. Lassiter will be well taken care of."

It was twilight by the time the three men had dug all around the base of the pine tree with the slash marks. Then they dug random shallow trenches all across the small clearing. But they didn't find a trace of the funds that Xavier Betain had sent north for his wayward son.

A moon had risen by the time they filled in all the holes and trenches and were riding back to Sunrise. McKenzie wasn't in his office but was taking supper at Lordine's. Telfont escorted the girl to the cafe, set her down at a table, then went to get the sheriff who was hunched over a plate at the counter. McKenzie, frowning, brought his dinner over to the table and sat down. He gave Ivy Eading a nod and then, at Telfont's prompting, she told her story.

"I'm going after Lassiter," Telfont said. "I'll bring him in."

"Now, wait a minute—"

"Betain must have got in a lucky shot before he was killed. Anyhow, Lassiter's leaking a lot of blood. No matter what he was, Betain didn't deserve to be shot down like a dog."

"A lot of folks around here might not agree with you," the sheriff said grimly.

"Because of the railroad. Yeah, I know, Ian, but from what I understand, Betain was on the verge of getting new financing. Which would have made a lot of people happy, you included."

"Yeah, I put money in his damned scheme," McKenzie admitted.

"Lassiter will be easy to track, especially with the shape he's in. Joe Gilbey could follow those blood spots with his eyes shut."

While McKenzie sat hunched in the cafe chair, bearded chin sunk in his chest, Telfont got to his feet, catching Ivy by her wrist and pulling her up.

"With Betain dead, it doesn't look like anybody will get money out of the Sunrise Valley Railroad," Telfont said. "Not now."

McKenzie's beard pushed even deeper against his broad chest. "Damn if it don't look that way, Marcus," he said dolefully.

Telfont walked Ivy over to the Dover Store. Dover, who was just closing up, heard the story of how she had gone riding that day and by chance witnessed a gruesome murder.

McKenzie finally roused himself after several minutes spent reflecting on past mistakes of a financial nature. He thought of going out for Betain's body, then decided to wait until daylight—and at the same time he'd talk Marcus Telfont out of going after Lassiter. McKenzie would organize his own group but if Telfont wanted to go along, well, it was all right, he guessed.

As it turned out, Telfont didn't wait until morning. He and Gilbey and others took the Lassiter trail that night.

Within an hour a rainstorm whipped up over the mountains and drenched the lowlands. They had to take shelter in a grove of trees, huddled in their slickers.

That night Ivy Eading lay in her bed, unable to sleep. Visions of what she had witnessed that day kept storming through her weary mind. She had left her horse back in the trees when she'd seen Lassiter and Betain turn off the road. But by the time she had crept forward on foot toward the sound of the voices, the shooting had started.

Terrified, she'd begun to run. But then to her right she saw Betain staggering off into the pines. And the next thing she knew Telfont and his men were charging through the trees, yelling. Down a lane of pines she had a clear view of Betain slumped on the ground and Telfont standing over him with a gun. Then there'd been enraged voices, a gunshot, and Betain had lain dead.

If she told it the way Telfont wanted it would be a lie. And the two things in the world she hated most

CHAPTER THIRTEEN

Lassiter worried when Victoria didn't return from her hasty trip up to Shelby's Point. When he got up, the room swam and dizziness drove him back to the sofa. There he sat, breathing hard, trying to collect his wits. The next time he tried to walk to the front window, he made it.

He stared out at the miles and miles of trees and jagged cliffs. Nothing moved except a mountain goat climbing on a ledge of rock above the mine tunnel.

Just when he was about to go and saddle up and try to find her, Victoria rode in. She came up the long stairway at a run, two steps at a time. He opened the door for her and saw below her saddle horse and the pack mule she had taken.

She whipped off her hat and her red-gold hair came tumbling about her flushed face. "I've got news," she panted. "Not good."

"Tell me," he said tensely.

"They say you killed Betain. Murdered him. There's a posse trying to track you."

Lassiter squeezed his eyes to slits. "Murdered Betain? Hell, he was alive the last I saw him."

"Nevertheless, they say you did it."

"How are they so sure?"

"Some girl is said to have witnessed it."

"All she has to do is tell the truth—"

"Obviously she isn't. The man who brought the news was carrying the mail. He came on ahead of the posse. Lassiter, you've got to get out of here."

He leaned a hand against the wall to take the strain off his weakened legs. "So as not to bring trouble to you. Yeah, I can see that."

His mind was spinning in turmoil. The smart thing, he knew, was to return to Sunrise, tell the truth of the encounter with Betain and get it over with. But her next words chilled that possibility.

"According to the bearer of grim tidings," she said with a twist of her lovely lips, "Telfont says he'll see you hang for killing such an outstanding citizen as Corse Betain." She threw her hands toward the smoke-blackened ceiling. "Can you imagine that? Outstanding citizen. My God, they nearly killed him because of the funds he embezzled. Now Telfont tries to say he's . . ." She broke off, shaking her head. "It doesn't make sense."

"Telfont again, eh?" His voice was cold.

But her voice held a note of excitement. "I've got to get you into the next territory—"

"I go alone," he snapped.

"The very hell with that suggestion." She gripped him by the arms, peering up into his face. "You can't go alone. We go together!"

He tried to appeal to the rational side of her mind. "You can't just walk out and leave your mine."

"It'll be here. When and if I come back." Her gray eyes were shining, the full lips curved into a smile. "Listen, Lassiter. I've lived in these mountains off and on since I was fourteen. I know every square foot of them. I know secret trails the Indians used. I can get you away when no one else can."

His weakened legs gave way and he had to sit down. He was too weary to argue with her but he did ask one serious question. "You sure you don't hold it against me for what they say I did to Betain?"

"Hold it against you? If you shot him as they say you did, I rejoice. Even if you did kill him."

That surprised him.

"Usually I place great value on human life. But not in this case," she went on.

"Tell me why?" he asked, sensing he was on the verge of learning a great truth.

"Because I was married to the bastard!" she fairly shouted. "You've done me the greatest favor possible. You made me a widow!"

"Married to him. So that's what was between you two." He gave her a long look. "You sure must've kept it a secret."

"It was his wish. He married me for the mine. Then he decided it wasn't worth the bother because by then he had the idea for the railroad. He had visions of being the big man of the valley, a bigger man than his father by far. He asked me not to divorce him until the railroad was built. Like a fool I agreed."

"You owed him that much?"

"At first we had some good times." Her mouth

tightened. "He could be charming. And then again he could be the very devil."

She made Lassiter rest while she carried up half the supplies she had purchased at Shelby's Point. The rest they would take with them. Again he tried to argue her out of accompanying him, but she refused to listen. He was too weak to pursue the matter. Whenever he thought of Telfont's threat to see him hang, a coldness rippled along his spine.

She doctored his wound with arnica she had purchased and gave him laudanum. In a closet she found an old shirt and jacket that had belonged to her late uncle. He had been a shorter man and grossly overweight. Even then the clothing was almost too tight.

When she had saddled his horse and they were ready to ride, she locked up the house and helped him down the flight of stairs.

"I wish you'd stay behind," he said again.

"And throw you to the hangman? I owe you, Lassiter, for quite possibly delivering me from a cold-hearted husband."

"But I didn't kill him," he said in a strained voice. "I keep telling you that."

She flashed her strong teeth in a smile and put her attention to helping him mount his black horse. At first as he settled in his saddle the mountain seemed to tilt dangerously and he was afraid of falling. He had to grip the saddlehorn with both hands. But gradually the mountain steadied.

"Are you all right?" she called anxiously. He nodded his head.

As they passed the barn, the mules started braying. "What about them?" Lassiter asked. His tongue seemed to have acquired a new thickness.

"I'm going to stop off near the point. I'll leave word with Dan Weaver. He'll take care of them for me."

He didn't say anything. The sway of the horse spread pain along his lacerated side. He had to bite his lips to keep from crying out.

On the outskirts of the Point she left him with the pack mule in the trees and galloped up a long hillside toward a small cabin set on a ledge of rock. He drooped in the saddle, watching her from under his hat brim. Her figure swam in his vision. He thought of the day he'd appropriated the brown horse for Betain and had returned to find the man lying on the ground. The thought crossed Lassiter's mind that he might suffer the same fate if he let himself go for even a moment.

After what seemed like an age, she returned. "Dan will do it," she announced. "Keep an eye on the place and care for the stock."

He barely heard her. After a few miles he was aware that he no longer held the reins, she did. She was leading his black horse up the face of the mountain on a steep zig-zag trail. A cold wind tore at his breath and watered his eyes.

Through his feverish mind stormed the incongruity of Victoria, young and attractive and intelligent, allowing a man like Corse Betain to shackle her with a wedding ring. Then he thought back to his own involvement with the man. Hadn't he tried to shield him? To take his part against others who had condemned him. Hadn't Xavier Betain in one of the last statements of his life said fervently that his only son needed help? If grown men could be taken in then why not a young and inexperienced woman?

At last they came to the road again and soon in the distance he could see a few scattered shacks. She said it was a mountain settlement that they would avoid. A stranger and a known resident of the mountains and mine owner being seen together would be remembered if and when a posse asked questions.

Hooves rattled on stone as the horses and the mule labored ever upward.

Leaning over in the saddle, after they had passed the hamlet, she pressed a hand against his forehead. She bit her lip. "You're feverish. Oh Lord, you should be home in bed and not up here in the peaks with an icy wind blowing."

"I'll survive." He gave a weak smile. "With your help."

"You have my help," she assured him instantly.

It was nearly dark when he was awakened from a half sleep by the crack of a rifle. His mouth dried as his eyes flew open. He was still sitting his saddle, but the reins of the black horse were trailed and Victoria was gone. He turned cold, thinking she might be in trouble. But she wasn't. She had shot an antelope for their supper.

But when she had roasted the meat over an open fire, he found he wasn't hungry. She made him some broth and he managed to get some of it down.

The next day, because they were some distance from the road, she let him sleep till noon. He awakened fairly refreshed.

"Did you ever sleep," she said with a smile.

"Guess I needed it."

"Your voice is stronger."

Not only his voice but his strength had returned. No longer did the ground tilt. He rolled his own blankets and tied them on behind the cantle. But by then he was winded.

"Don't try to do too much," she cautioned.

The next day she scouted ahead and returned looking worried. She said that a body of riders had passed within a quarter of a mile from where she'd watched from a stand of aspen.

"Telfont?" he asked numbly.

"Maybe. But I couldn't be sure. We'll change directions to throw them off. If indeed they are after us."

"Me, you mean. Not us. Victoria, I've got my strength back. I think you oughta head back for the mine."

But she refused to hear of it on two counts. One, she wanted to stay with him. And her eyes took on a strange glow when she said it. And two, he wasn't as strong as he pretended to be.

When they stopped again and dismounted, he found he could step down without his knees threatening to cave in on him. She caught his hands and rubbed them vigorously between her own.

"They're icy," she said, then thrust them under her jacket and close to her warm body. A flicker of desire touched him as he felt the swell of her breasts against his hands.

A great *V* of wild geese cut across the blue dome of the sky, on their way north for the summer. Later they stood on a ledge and saw a great grizzly in a grassy cut far below. It came to its hind legs, sniffed the air, then turned and ambled quickly out of sight. But no sign of pursuit.

"We've been moving so slowly I'm sure they've passed us," she said. "But the last sign I saw of them, they were still heading west. We cut across their trail again about five miles back."

"You know how to read sign," he marveled. "I never knew a woman who could."

"Perhaps I have other hidden attributes." She cocked a reddish brow and smiled at him. He smiled back. He was definitely feeling better. That evening he had more broth made from the chunks of antelope meat she'd brought along. Their fire was small, barely enough to cook the meat and heat the broth, and was not likely to call attention to them.

He was curious about her marriage to Corse Betain.

She gave a short laugh, cradling a tin coffee cup in her shapely hands as she sat cross-legged on the ground. Behind her the shadows were thick. The fire snapped and crackled. The aroma of broiled antelope meat lingered in the air.

"With Corse not wanting the marriage to be known, we soon had the reputation of living in sin." She laughed again. "Which he did actually later down in Sunrise, so I was given to understand. With Etta Dempster."

Lassiter felt his earlobes grow warm as he recalled his own brief association with the voluptuous brunette.

"If what they say is true," she went on wistfully, "that Corse is dead, then it's the second time I've been a widow."

He looked in surprise at her shadowed face. "A widow . . . twice?"

"My father was one of the first casualties of the war. My poor mother wanted me to be safe, so she arranged for me to marry a Lieutenant Stanhope. I was fourteen and he was twenty-seven. He was captured by the Confederates and died in Libby Prison."

"Poor Victoria," he murmured.

"I barely knew him. We only had one week together. I had hoped my second marriage would prove more durable. For one thing, I was no longer a child. And Corse was only a few years older; there wasn't thirteen years difference as in my first marriage. . . ."

He fell asleep sitting up. She pulled off his boots as she had been doing each night and helped him into his blankets, then went to her own bed.

In the morning he was determined to saddle his own horse. By the time it was done he was damp with cold sweat. But his wound no longer pained him to the point of nausea and collapse.

"I did it," he announced triumphantly.

"Soon you'll be a whole man," she said with a mysterious smile. Walking to her horse, she looked back at him over her shoulder, a strange gleam in her gray eyes.

A few miles west there was another camp in a valley where the wind had swept the night sky free of clouds so that the stars seemed close enough to be touched by a jumping man. A three-quarter moon bathed great domes of granite in a yellow glow. Night birds were busy in the trees and there was the restless stomp of hobbled horses.

Telfont whittled on a stick as he sat before a roaring fire. Sparks danced skyward. He thrust a long twig into the fire and when it was flaming used it to light a cigarette. He stared at the flaming twig for a long minute.

"I've heard that if you shove something like this under an hombre's fingernail he'll tell you most anything you want to hear." Telfont gave a mirthless chuckle. "Lassiter I'm talking about."

"I've got a better idea," Joe Gilbey growled from where he lay on his side a few feet away. "Peel off his britches an' set him on hot coals."

Red Shanley said, "I'm glad Joe ain't after *me*."

"Lassiter knocked some skin off Joe's knuckles," Telfont said. "So you can't blame him for wanting to get even."

"Not only that, he slammed me on the jaw," Gilbey said sourly.

Jud Ream sat up and said in his powerful voice, "How much money you reckon Lassiter's got hid away, anyhow?"

Telfont turned his head and looked at Ream's heavy figure in the shadows. He didn't like it that Ream was so curious. After it was all over with, Ream just might fill the hole where the money had been buried. Not even a mound to mark his grave. Maybe a little something green sprouting from the breastbone come spring. Telfont smiled coldly at the idea.

"How much longer you figure they're gonna give us the slip?" Gilbey wanted to know.

"Victoria knows the mountains, so I've been given to understand," Telfont said. He dropped the burning twig back into the fire where it was instantly consumed. "She's the one directing the game."

"She oughta pay for givin' us so much trouble," Gilbey said with heat in his voice.

"Naturally I'll have first go at her," Telfont said softly. "The rest of you can flip a coin."

Red Shanley cleared his throat nervously. "What you reckon Lassiter'll say about that."

"He won't have a good goddammed thing to say." Telfont leaned forward to stare at Shanley whose blotched face was highlighted by the flames of the cook fire. "By then he'll have told it all and even drawn a map to show just where the money is buried."

"He's got a reputation as a tricky son of a bitch," Shanley said. "Was it me, I'd ride him back down an' make him dig up the money hisself."

"Well, maybe," Telfont conceded. "I don't want to get too close to town with him and run into McKenzie, maybe. And have the damned sheriff take him off our hands."

Telfont rolled up in his blankets, having a feeling that tomorrow would see the business with Lassiter at an end. But it didn't turn out that way. His mood worsened and he barely spoke to the other three all day.

CHAPTER FOURTEEN

The next afternoon Victoria and Lassiter saw a small cabin nearly hidden in a thick grove of aspen on a ledge halfway up a hillside. You had to look quick or miss it altogether.

"Wonder if anybody's home?" Lassiter speculated, his forearms crossed on the saddlehorn as he stared up the hillside; by then he was so weary he wondered if he could continue for many more miles.

"I remember it," Victoria said. "A line shack."

The place had been boarded up for the winter, not used since the previous fall. It wouldn't be opened again until late spring when all the snows were gone and the cattle could be driven to this elevation for mountain grass.

He sat slumped in the saddle while she went around the small building, stooping and turning over loose boards and stones. Finally she gave a triumphant cry and appeared, brandishing a large key.

When she had the place open, he dropped into a big chair with leather straps for the seat. Although he was about done in after the long day, he helped her put up the horses and mule in a small barn and feed them with hay left in the bin.

The only food in the line shack were some dried onions. Victoria took her rifle and slipped out into the twilight. Presently there was a rifle shot. Lassiter straightened in the chair, his Henry across his lap. But she came in with a haunch of venison wrapped in a piece of tarp she had found in the barn.

"Now we eat," she announced and got busy with a sharp knife.

That evening he found that his appetite had finally returned. And when they were eating he said it was by far the best meal he'd ever had in his life.

"Only venison and onions," she pointed out, but was pleased by his compliment.

After the meal, they went to a creek nearby where the deer had come to drink. There they scoured the tin plates with sand and rinsed them. She returned them to the cupboard.

Even though they had built a fire, an icy wind howled through the cracks in the line shack's walls.

"We'll need each other for warmth tonight," she said, giving him a level look. "It'll be freezing cold up here and we don't have enough blankets."

Despite the harrowing experience he had undergone, he felt himself looking forward to her suggestion.

In the narrow lower bunk her body felt warm and soft against his. At first he felt only a flickering desire but it began to grow, steady as a candle flame moved out of a stiffening breeze. She lay in the crook of his right arm, her hair silken against her cheek.

His fingers started making circles up and down her back until she began to toss about. Then she sat up, bumping her head on the bottom of the upper bunk. She gave a strangled little laugh, swore softly and began to struggle out of her clothing. Then, under the blankets, she again came into his arms. He resumed the caresses, exploring a curved hip until he finally reached the soft flesh of her inner thighs. By then she was moving against him on the narrow bunk and making soft noises as if in her sleep.

But asleep she was not, for when he looked down he saw one large gray eye watching him and a half smile on her moistly parted lips.

"You lie still," she whispered, "and I'll be ever so careful of your poor ribs on the left side."

"There's isn't room," he protested weakly, but fired by desire nevertheless. "You'll bump your head again."

"So I bump my head," she said. In a few seconds he found himself encircled by incredible warmth. He clutched at her soft shoulders as he soared to impossible heights.

During the night a storm swept in, and rain and hail pelted the roof. It leaked. But the upper bunk was protection.

In the morning they lay in each other's arms again. During the night more of his strength had returned and this time he directed their lovemaking.

For breakfast they had venison and onions again, laughing like two children on a forbidden picnic.

After leaving the cabin as they had found it and returning the key to a flat stone, they rode out. It was a beautiful morning. Up ahead a few snowdrifts had been hammered relentlessly by last night's rain. Everything seemed green and sparkling. To the west a few frothy clouds hovered above some sawtooth peaks.

They crossed a great high valley with a floor of rock and sparse vegetation. Now that his mind was clear once again and his body stronger, he kept looking to their backtrail. But nothing moved behind them except once when a herd of antelope leaped from cover. And then with the natural curiosity of the breed, the animals halted on a rise of ground to watch them. Just before noon they saw a brown bear and two cubs at a distance. And they could not help but hear the great roar of the protective mother, warning them to stay away from her young.

For their noon meal they nibbled cold venison and then had it warmed over a low fire for supper. While she prepared the meal he cleared a space of stones and twigs for their blankets. No longer was there any pretense; he made a single bed. This time she cried out finally in ecstasy; his cry was partly from the pain brought on by his exertion.

But the pain soon passed. The ground was hard and cold but their entwined limbs protected them from the night chill. In the morning he awakened, his body stiff. There was only a slight stain on the fresh bandage she had applied.

"You're better than any doctor," he complimented and found her eager lips.

At noon he circled back to a high point of land to study the rough country they had crossed, the miles of trees, the giant rocks at the base of the cliffs where patches of snow lingered on into the spring. A dot of movement far off caught his eye.

"Somebody coming," he rasped, catching up to her and the pack mule. "We better get out of this open country and back into the trees."

They started hurrying down a long slope of shale that put a stain of dust into the air. He groaned in dismay and grit his teeth, but it couldn't be helped. If someone spotted their dust it would just have to be. But within an hour they were crossing a long, grassy valley and the telltale dust had vanished.

Late in the day they came to a settlement known as Hesper, a collection of log buildings at the tag end of nowhere with tight-lipped inhabitants who regarded them suspiciously. Obviously they saw few strangers.

After spotting a hotel and cafe Victoria said they should take the risk and sleep "civilized," as she put it with a merry laugh.

They got a hotel room and put up the horses and mule in a livery barn. Victoria went to the store to pick up a few things she wanted. While she was gone, he sat on the edge of the bed in their room. Just as he leaned down to pull off his boots, the door began to open. Still a little fuzzy, he managed a welcoming smile.

But it wasn't Victoria who stood in the doorway. His smile froze into the face of Marcus Telfont. He twisted around on the bed, ready to leap for a window, but Joe Gilbey stood in the alley with a rifle. Gilbey's grin said he'd welcome resistance.

In Lassiter's still-weakened condition, he was no match for the two men who swarmed over him and pinned him to the bed. Telfont was leaning against the wall, looking on, an amused smile on his lips. Red Shanley and Jud Ream were holding Lassiter by the arms.

"Where's the woman?" Telfont asked in a hard voice.

"She left me miles back."

"We'll see." He called Gilbey into the room. "Joe, you know Victoria Reed by sight. This is a small town. Go find her."

Gilbey's eyes lighted in anticipation. "Hey, it won't seem near so long goin' back as it did comin' up. With her along for . . . company." He leered at Lassiter and left the room. Lassiter could hear his heavy footsteps in the hall.

"Listen to me," Lassiter said tensely. "She had nothing to do with my troubles."

"She helped a fugitive escape," Telfont said with a superior smile.

"I know what you want and I'm willing to give it to you." Lassiter's blue eyes locked with Telfont's amber. "Just let her go."

"What are you willing to give?" Telfont asked softly.

"What Xavier Betain gave me to bring to his son."

Telfont looked thoughtful. The tip of his tongue moved slowly along the underside of his ragged, no longer fashionably waxed mustache.

"All right, tell me," he said.

"Send these two out of the room. The fewer know

about this the better." Lassiter managed to keep his voice from cracking with strain. It was a gamble, but the only course he had to try and save Victoria.

"I see," Telfont mused.

Lassiter could almost read his mind. Telfont and Lassiter to go back over the mountains, the other three left behind. Lassiter, a prisoner, to dig up the money. Telfont to end it with a bullet and have the money without splitting it with Gilbey or anyone else.

"Get a pencil and paper," Lassiter urged breathlessly. If he could only get Shanley and Ream out of the room he'd make his move against Telfont. "I'll draw you a map, then just the two of us . . ." He let it hang there while Telfont seemed to consider the proposition.

Shanley's sun-blotched face darkened. "He's a tricky son of a bitch. Remember me tellin' you that?"

"Yeah," Telfont grunted and some of the tension went out of his shoulders. "As long as you're in the mood to draw a map, Lassiter," Telfont said, "do it!" He took a short letter from his coat pocket. It was written only on one side. With a pencil Telfont made a large X through the handwriting and turned the letter over to the blank side.

"Turn him loose," he instructed the two men. "Let him draw the map."

Lassiter fought down his disappointment when Telfont didn't dismiss the pair from the room. But there was still a chance, he told himself. As the men released his arms, he started toward the rickety table where Telfont had placed the paper and pencil.

Hoping Telfont wouldn't notice that he was reaching for the pencil with his left hand, he suddenly spun and with his right grabbed the butt of Red Shanley's holstered gun. He had it half-drawn from the leather when Ream slammed into him from behind. The force of Ream's powerful shoulder knocked Lassiter against the wall and tore his hand away from Shanley's gun.

There was a simultaneous metallic clicking as the weapons of the three men were cocked and pointed. Lassiter stiffened.

And at that moment the door was thrust open and Victoria stood white-faced in the opening. Behind her was Joe Gilbey, a pleased smile on his savage face.

He pushed Victoria into the room and closed the door at his back.

"Oh, Lassiter, I'm so sorry," she said in a stricken voice. Her gray eyes were filled with pain and she kept biting her lips.

"Let's get out of here," Telfont snapped. He produced a pair of manacles. Despite his weakness, it took three of them to hold Lassiter facedown on the bed so his wrists could be manacled. When Victoria tried to leap to his aid, Gilbey slapped her hard across the face. She turned on him, nails like claws, but Gilbey ducked, got behind her and gripped her slender wrists in one powerful hand.

"You go on ahead, Marcus," Gilbey said, panting. "This honey was gonna claw my face. I'm gonna fix her . . ."

"I should let you have your way," Telfont said coldly. "All the damned trouble she's caused us. But there'll be plenty of time once we're out of town."

When Lassiter and Victoria were pushed out into

the sorry main street of Hester, a few people gathered to stare at them curiously.

"Please help us," Victoria cried, but Telfont cut her off.

"This man," meaning Lassiter, "is a murderer. We're taking him back to Sunrise for trial."

"He'll never get there alive and you know it!" Victoria sobbed; great tears were running down her cheeks. One cheek was bright red where Gilbey had slapped her.

They were just about to ride out when Joe Gilbey swore and said, "Looky behind us, Marcus."

Telfont turned in the saddle and tried not to show his surprise and anger at the unwelcome sight of Ian McKenzie's bearded face. With the stern-looking sheriff were six townsmen from Sunrise, among them Doc Maydon.

"Well, Ian, you've come quite a ways," Telfont said with a forced smile.

"When I found out you'd left town, I picked up your tracks. You sure as hell led us all over hell's half acre."

"It was the Reed girl did it," Telfont said. "She knows these mountains—"

"No matter. We found you . . . in time." He looked significantly at Telfont. "Let's get on the move."

"Listen to me, Sheriff," Lassiter said from the saddle of his black horse. "I didn't kill Corse Betain—"

"A jury'll decide that."

Victoria spoke through clenched teeth. "Telfont and his men intended to rape me."

The sheriff stiffened. "How do you know that?"

Telfont managed to look at her in dismay. "Miss

Reed, how can you even *think* we'd be so inhuman?"

The sheriff turned to Victoria and said grimly, "I suggest you make your way back to your mine. It'll save possible . . . complications if you ain't along with us."

Then he gave the order to move out. Again Victoria appealed to the citizens of Hesper but they wanted no part of a stranger's troubles.

The posse finally stopped to let the horses blow. Gilbey, in his frustration, backhanded Lassiter across the face.

"We'll have none of that!" Doc Maydon warned, shoving his horse between the two mounts. "He goes back in one piece."

Telfont gave the raging Gilbey a faint shake of the head. Swearing under his breath, Gilbey reined aside.

The way back was much swifter than the pace Lassiter and Victoria had maintained. When they stopped at dark and ate their meager rations, the doctor came to sit at Lassiter's side. Two men with rifles stood at Lassiter's back. He was sitting on the ground, legs outstretched, a chunk of greasy antelope steak in his hand. The manacles had been removed but they had made deep indentations in his wrists. As he chewed, he worried about Victoria.

"I'm counting on you to present a creditable defense," the doctor said above the crackle of the dying cook fire.

"All I've got is my word that I didn't do it."

The doctor looked at him in the shadows. There was a faint glow from the bowl of his pipe against the gray stubble on his chin. "I was hoping you might have a witness."

Lassiter gave a short laugh. "I have. Telfont. And I think I recognized Gilbey's voice. Probably Shanley and the big one along with them."

"Getting them to tell the truth will take some doing," Doc Maydon said with a shake of his head.

"Some way I'll manage."

"I hope so, Lassiter." The doctor got to his feet. "It's been a long trail for a man of my years. I better get some sleep."

"I'm glad you came along, Doc," Lassiter said sincerely.

"I was afraid Telfont and his cronies might use bad judgment and you wouldn't arrive back in Sunrise at all. And I wasn't too sure of our estimable sheriff," he added in a low voice.

A low growling sound came from Telfont, who sat cross-legged a few feet away in deep shadow. "That was unnecessary, Doc, to say that about me. And my friends."

"I know what happens sometimes when a posse goes after a suspected murderer," the doctor said. "When I was a young man I was with such a posse. The suspect never lived to get a fair trial. I didn't want to risk having it happen again is all."

It was long past midnight when Lassiter awakened, a hand on his shoulder, another hand lightly across his mouth. He lifted his head and by the last embers of the cook fire recognized Telfont.

"Easy, Lassiter," Telfont hissed. "I want to talk about money."

"There is no money. I was lying back at the hotel."

"Miss Eading swears she overheard you and Betain arguing about money."

"Who's she?"

Telfont seemed to realize he had let something slip he hadn't intended. "Lassiter, I'll arrange for you to escape," Telfont went on in that deep whisper, his lips close to Lassiter's ear.

"Then what?"

"We find the money. We split. And you can be on your way."

"What about the murder charge?" Lassiter whispered back, watching as much of the shadowed face as he could see.

"I'll take care of that."

Lassiter's smile was ugly. "I'll stake my life on the truth coming out at the trial."

"Then you're a fool." Telfont was losing patience. "Better to take a chance with me than go out with a rope around your neck."

Lassiter's wrists were manacled again, this time in front. His weight was supported by his elbows. A dry stick crackled in the fire and a galaxy of embers shot skyward. There were snores from the sleeping posse-men. Some of them snorted and twisted in their sleep.

"Telfont, I wouldn't trust you any farther than I could spit with the wind in my face."

"This is your last chance, dammit!"

Telfont's voice was raised in anger and some of the nearby heads came up. "What's goin' on?" one of them said.

"Nothing," Telfont snapped and stomped over to his own blankets.

Lassiter stayed awake for a long time, staring at the stars overhead. A name kept spinning around in his head. Miss Eading. Then, suddenly, he remembered. She was the new blond clerk at the Dover Store, the one everybody was talking about. If she had been present to witness Betain talking about the money, then she must have also witnessed the shootout. He finally fell asleep, a faint smile on his lips.

CHAPTER FIFTEEN

The following day, as they descended a long, grassy slope past clumps of aspen and juniper, Lassiter managed to ride side by side with the doctor. In a low voice he told him about Telfont.

"I'll talk to Miss Eading myself," the doctor promised.

"Much thanks, Doc."

"I don't understand her position at the store. Surely Wilbur doesn't need extra help. Can't understand why he hired her in the first place." The doctor was silent as their horses made a few paces through the grass, then he said, "Well I guess I do understand, at that." He gave a mirthless chuckle.

Word of the posse's return swept the town of Sunrise with the speed of a lightning-set summer fire in dry brush. Both sides of the street were lined when Lassiter was ridden into town. To avoid too much of a crowd, Sheriff McKenzie planned to slip Lassiter into jail by the alley door.

He dismounted and hammered on the heavy door. "It's McKenzie, Dirk! Open up!"

They heard the sound of double bars being withdrawn from metal slots. Then the door swung open. Heavy-muscled Dirk Foley, a deputy-sheriff badge on his stained brown vest, grinned at the sheriff. "I see you run the bastard down."

McKenzie grunted something and shoved Lassiter into the building. A chill clung to the stone walls and the heavy wood planks of the floor. It had rained that morning and a cold wind was sweeping down from the mountains. There was only one other prisoner in the jail and he was in a cell at the far end of the corridor. A drunk, from the crazy way he was singing to himself. Aside from the chill dampness, the air was filled with the odors of stale food and urine.

In a large end-cell McKenzie unlocked the manacles from Lassiter's wrists. Lassiter stood rubbing the circulation back into his arms. "I want to see a lawyer, McKenzie."

"Ain't but one. Heck Orley." The sheriff locked the cell door and gave Lassiter a speculative look through the bars. "To tell the truth, when I heard they'd gone after you, I never figured to see you back here. Unless it was dead and you was draped over the back of a hoss."

"Thanks for taking the trouble to hunt for me," Lassiter said. "Now about this lawyer . . ."

But McKenzie had walked away. Lassiter could hear his boots echoing on the plank floor. A door opened and closed. All that remained was the voice of the drunk coming faintly from the other end of the building.

Lassiter walked over and looked out his cell window. It opened onto an alley. He tested the bars. They were thick and solidly set into holes that had been drilled into the stone wall. He'd prove his innocence, he vowed. Either that or somehow he'd break out of this stone trap.

At the town of Hesper Victoria Reed sold the mule and the cooking gear and started out on what she planned to be a fast trip. Although the posse was traveling at a good pace, she passed them by half a mile when they made camp for the night. She pushed on, straining her eyes in the light of a feeble moon to keep her horse away from danger. It would have been smarter to have kept the mule, she supposed, because it was more sure-footed in the mountains. But at the time she had been too upset to think logically.

When she finally reached her mine, she was so weary that after caring for the tired horse, she flung herself into bed, a bed she had not expected to see again for a long time, if ever. In the back of her mind she had thought that she and Lassiter would just keep on going. Maybe all the way to San Francisco where they would start new lives.

And now thanks to that bastard Telfont, it could all be over. She thought longingly of Lassiter's embrace. How wrong some people were about him. He was a warm and sympathetic man, not an icicle with a killer's mind.

Down in Sunrise, Ivy Eading was also thinking of Lassiter. Would a rope around his neck make up for him killing Charlie? At first she had been so positive that any kind of revenge would be sweet. She had ridden endless miles, risked all kinds of trouble, just to bring that about. And here in Sunrise everything had finally fallen right into her lap.

She lay on her side in Marcus Telfont's large bed. Telfont had his back turned. She could hear his steady breathing. Tonight, when he had called for her, Wilbur Dover had not taken it gracefully. His face had twisted and he'd muttered at Telfont, who had only smiled tolerantly and pushed him away.

In the store, her heart pounding, she had wanted to turn her back on Telfont. But she was afraid of him; he seemed so overpowering. He was arrogant and had no consideration for anybody. She knew he was using her but didn't know how to get out of it. If she complained to Wilbur Dover she might only succeed in getting the little merchant killed. She'd already had enough death in her life.

But on the other hand, had Charlie been so much different from Telfont? She wondered, thinking of the nights she had lain awake while Charlie was off playing cards or up to some mischief with his friend Chick. When he finally did come home, usually just before dawn and smelling of whiskey and occasionally cheap perfume, he would take what he thought was his due then curl up and go to sleep. She would be left in wretched loneliness.

Had she been blind all those days since he had been killed? Was avenging Charlie her way of heaping all the injustice done to her into one big package and destroying it? She had given that package a name: Lassiter.

She heard Telfont grunt in his sleep. She felt one of his hands move over her. She pretended to be asleep, but it was too late.

As she stared up at the pale blue ceiling, now in

shadow and not looking at all like the sky, she recalled how Charlie used to tease her. One time he had said with his lazy wink, "The day they passed out the brains, you was down to the creek washin' out your underwear."

Maybe Charlie had been right; she just wasn't too bright.

Then she stiffened and clenched her hands. No, she told herself, she was as smart as anybody. Her trouble was that she was just too trusting. Too afraid of some people.

Telfont said, "What's the matter?"

"N-n-nothing."

"You got all tense there for a minute."

"Did I?"

Then Telfont continued with what he was doing and soon it was dawn.

The next day he called for her at Dover's and gave her a large package. It was a blue silk dress that he said would match her eyes. She tried to show her appreciation. Dover glowered and his heavyset wife looked pleased.

That evening Telfont took her to the hotel for dinner. She felt uncomfortable with so many people staring at her. But Telfont seemed oblivious to their stares. He ordered fresh trout and wine.

"That blue dress shows off your hair," Telfont said gallantly. "In fact, with your hair pinned up you look positively regal."

If the compliment had come from anyone else she might have been flattered. But the way Telfont looked at her out of his amber eyes made her cringe.

They were just finishing their supper when Etta Dempster entered with a tall, rawboned rancher.

Leaving her escort, Etta came gliding across the crowded dining room, her dress rustling.

A stiff smile was on her lips but the black eyes had the devil in them. "Marcus dear, I see you have your peasant of the week with you."

"Etta, Etta," Telfont said, getting to his feet.

"I understand there's to be a hanging in two weeks," Etta said in an icily pleasant voice.

"Perhaps," Telfont said.

"Oh, there will be." Her laughter was brittle as she gave Ivy a look, then crossed the room. Her tall rancher, red-faced at Etta's loud voice, was holding a chair for her.

"Etta's a once-rich girl who's already spent the money her father left," Telfont explained. "And now she's trying to take it out on the world. Pay no attention to the bitch."

"I felt like slapping her face," Ivy said, and Telfont laughed.

In front of the hotel Telfont tried to talk Ivy into going home with him again. But this time she declined. He argued, then gave up. "Don't forget you're going to testify for the prosecution."

"I . . . I'll have to think about it. . . ."

He grabbed her arm and walked her swiftly to a corner of the street where the trees and other buildings threw deep shadows. There he twisted her arm up behind her back like Charlie used to do when he was drunk or angry. The pain made her cry out.

"You've given your word that you'll testify," Telfont said in a low, dangerous voice. "Don't go back on it, my dear."

His eyes lanced coldly into her face, causing her

to shiver. Finally she nodded her head. "Yes, I'll do what you want."

Only then did he release her arm and pat her on the cheek. "Sweet girl."

She winced at his touch.

That night she had a time falling asleep in her room behind the Dover Store. She thought of getting her horse from the livery barn and riding south. But even if she did, Telfont would run her down. She was convinced of it. And once he had threatened with a smile to turn her over to Joe Gilbey "if you're not a very good little girl."

Although it had been said supposedly in jest, the mere thought of Gilbey made her flesh crawl.

Then she forced her mind back to her original intention in coming to Sunrise. To avenge Charlie Baxter, wasn't that right? Of course, and once that was done she'd head back to Tucson so fast even the wind couldn't catch up to her.

CHAPTER SIXTEEN

Lassiter listened to the jibes from the crowd outside his cell window. "Betain was gonna git the damn railroad built after all, an' you had to go an' gun him down."

"I didn't have no love fer Betain," another man said, "but you shouldn't have kilt him."

"I didn't kill him," Lassiter responded patiently through the barred window. He lowered the window to cut the sound of their voices, but he could still hear them dimly and see the fists that were shaken at him.

He had two weeks before the judge arrived in town. But the next morning the sheriff came to tell him the time had been cut to one week. "Judge got through down the valley sooner than he figured. So you're in luck."

"Luck?" Lassiter laughed harshly. "I need to talk to the lawyer, damn it."

"I don't take no cussin' from prisoners!" McKenzie went tromping down the corridor and slammed the door to the jail office. He was thinking of Lassiter, almost pitying the man, when he stiffened. Through the window he saw Doc Maydon coming across the street. He groaned. The white-haired doctor was a persistent cuss and he dreaded seeing him.

Doc Maydon had just come from the Dover Store where he had tried to reason with Ivy Eading. But she told him she wasn't supposed to discuss the coming trial with anyone.

"I . . . I'm appearing for the prosecution," she said with a note almost of triumph, her blue eyes blazing.

Doc Maydon frowned, wondering what this slim blonde had against Lassiter, for it looked as though Ivy considered testifying against him a matter of vengeance.

The doctor entered the jail office and found McKenzie slouched in a chair, scowling at an old copy of a Denver paper that someone had left behind. He gave the doctor a spare nod.

"I'd like a few words with Lassiter," the doctor said.

But McKenzie, looking away, said that Lassiter was taking a nap.

"You mean Telfont told you to say that," Doc Maydon snapped. He had not fully recovered from the long trek into the mountains, and frustrations such as the one today with the Eading girl stretched his nerves.

What he had said about Telfont brought McKenzie roaring out of his varnished chair. "Where the hell do you get the idea that I listen to Telfont!"

"You better slow down, Ian," the doctor said calmly. "Your face is red as a mountain sunset. Bad for the heart."

Doc Maydon turned on his heel and left the jail office.

McKenzie plopped back into his chair, scowling. "Doc better keep his nose stuck in his medicine bag instead of pokin' it into other folks' business."

Dirk Foley entered the office in time to hear the last. A faint grin touched his long sun-browned face. "Hell, it'll all be over within a week."

"Yeah, guess it will." McKenzie stretched out his long legs and sighed.

"Who you gonna get for the hangman?"

"Hell, I even hate to think about it. I hate a hangin'. Me standin' on the scaffold tryin' to look important an' everybody starin' an' lookin' like they'll cheer the minute the poor bastard drops through the trap."

"A fine hangin' oughta be good for the town, Ian."

"I s'pose it'll bring folks in from the back country, once word gets out."

Foley strolled over to the front window and said, "Better keep your eye on Wilbur Dover."

"Why, for crissakes?"

"He's likely tryin' to figure a way to murder his wife," Foley answered, exposing his horse teeth in a big grin, "an' not git caught. So he can have that honey-headed female."

"How you know so much, Dirk?"

"Just seen 'em walk by. Ol' Wilbur patted her kinda low down when he figured nobody was lookin'."

"An' what'd she do?"

"Turned an' looked at him. Kinda hard like, seemed to me."

"Way I hear it," McKenzie said with a tight smile,

"Telfont's moved in on her. I don't figure Wilbur's got a prayer."

He fell to thinking again of the coming trial and the inevitable aftermath. "Reckon folks around here deserve a good show," he said to Foley, "an' that's what a hangin' really is. Somethin' to take their minds off all the money they put in Corse Betain's goddamn railroad." Including me, he almost said. He was thinking of the bundle of railroad stock certificates resting on a shelf in his small house at the edge of Sunrise. Thinking about it spoiled the rest of the evening for him.

When Lassiter's evening meal arrived from Lordine's Cafe, McKenzie grudgingly let the gaunt delivery man in.

It was over an hour later that Telfont crept into the alley behind the jail. He ignored a warning posted by Sheriff McKenzie about staring at the prisoner, and lifted one corner of the strip of heavy canvas that hung over the window.

He peered in at Lassiter slumped at a table, staring down at a dirty but empty plate. There was no knife, no fork, no chance for the prisoner to make any kind of weapon.

"I reckon you ate supper with your fingers," Telfont called softly through the window. "Want to talk to you."

Lassiter walked over to the window. "Now what?"

"I want to talk about money." Telfont's face was a blob of shadow behind the bars. He looked both ways along the alley. "I can get you out of here if you'll agree to the deal I offered up in the mountains."

"Get me out of here? How?"

"Never mind the details. It can be done. I've got Dirk Foley in my hind pocket." Telfont slapped at his backside for emphasis.

Lassiter wasn't too surprised that McKenzie's deputy might be Telfont's man. He shook his head. "I don't trust you worth a damn, Telfont."

Lassiter left the window and slumped again to the chair.

"It's your last chance, Lassiter. You've got no choice."

When Telfont, looking glum, went over to Teeley's for a drink, he found Doc Maydon the center of a group of men. The doctor was stressing his belief in the innocence of the accused. At that moment the doctor looked up and saw Telfont glaring at him.

"Justice will be done, Marcus," the doctor said, and everyone turned to look at Telfont to see how he was taking it.

Telfont lifted a shoulder, managed a smile. "Of course. Buy you a drink, Doc."

"Thanks, no." The doctor walked stiffly out of the saloon.

Frowning, Telfont ordered his private bottle.

Doc Maydon went to the alley behind the jail to have a few words with Lassiter through the cell window. But a strip of heavy canvas now covered the window on the outside. A notice fastened to the stone wall and signed by Sheriff McKenzie warned everyone to stay away from the window. And Dirk Foley was coming along the alley just then, carrying his ever-present sawed-off shotgun. Maydon hurried away.

Thoughtfully he walked home. He had a feeling in the pit of his stomach that it was all over for Lassiter.

At first he hadn't liked the man very much. Lassiter had seemed so sinister. And there was no denying he had a reputation, some of it good and some of it black as a stormy midnight. There were some folks who swore by him and others who swore at him. It depended on your dealings about the man, the doctor guessed. Be a friend and you'd get the same in return. But try to cross him and you'd find that Satan had teeth.

A day before the trial was to start, Doc Maydon was in Teeley's when a man entered, looked around, then shuffled over to where Doc was leaning against the bar, hat tipped back on his white head. Doc heard someone call his name. He looked around and saw the shabbily dressed man. He recognized him as a nester who lived out beyond Aspen Ridge.

"Doc, Jake sent me in to find you. Jake, he's my neighbor an' his wife is due. He wants you to come pronto."

"Jake who?"

"Strothers."

Doc Maydon was vaguely aware of the name. "You mean his wife is due to give birth?" And when the man nodded, the doctor mused, "I didn't even know she was pregnant."

"Wa'al, she sure is. Big as a country stove, she is. Looks to me like she's gonna have triplets."

"I see. You would know for sure, of course, being a graduate of medical school."

The wry humor was lost on the man. He stood at

the doctor's elbow, watching him out of small bright eyes.

Doc Maydon was staring out the window at the brightening day. It was so early that the soft hues of red and orange had barely left the eastern horizon. A stillness lay over Sunrise as if in anticipation of the important day tomorrow. Even the voices of the few drinkers in the saloon were hushed.

"How far is it out there?" the doctor asked, hating another long ride after the strenuous push over the mountains after Lassiter.

"You oughta be back by dark," the man said.

The doctor sighed. "Tell Jake Strothers I'll be out a little past noon."

"Sure will, Doc. An' I'm thankin' you."

A considerate neighbor, that nester, the doctor thought as he finished his drink.

Telfont was waiting behind the saloon. He listened to the shabbily dressed man relate what had transpired inside, then slipped him an eagle. The man clutched the gold coin in his grubby hand.

"Good work, Jethro," Telfont said in a dry voice. "Now make yourself scarce."

"Me belly's in need of whiskey." He grinned, scratching himself and eyeing the back windows of Teeley's.

"Not in there," Telfont warned roughly. "Do your drinking at Ben's down on Spruce Street."

"Will do that, Mr. Telfont, an' I'm obliged to you."

Telfont wrinkled his nose as the man shuffled away along the littered alley. Well, it was worth ten dollars to get the doctor out of the way. He wanted no protesting voices raised at the trial, and he knew that Doc's would likely be the loudest.

It was frustrating. He and Gilbey and the others had gone each day three miles east of town and dug up fresh patches of ground. But still no sign of the money. He had to get Lassiter over a barrel and was well on his way to doing it.

CHAPTER SEVENTEEN

During the long week in jail Lassiter's strength had nearly returned. He had chinned himself on the cross bar of his cell door, done jumping jacks and situps. Although he was winded after each session and the sweat poured out of him, he was beginning to feel revived.

Lassiter learned that on occasion some of the residents of the county thought he should be commended instead of tried for eliminating an embezzler like Corse Betain. But Telfont always seemed on hand to disagree. No man should take the law into his own hands, was Telfont's bland response.

Teeley's and the other two saloons in Sunrise were swarming with customers who had come in from the back country in anticipation of the trial and the hanging. A guilty verdict seemed to be a foregone conclusion.

Each time rumors of his demise on the gallows reached Lassiter he would turn cold for a minute or so before he was able to cast off the feeling of doom.

No, it couldn't be. A jury would find him innocent. On his lawyer's single visit to the jail, Lassiter had told him of Telfont's probable involvement in Betain's death. The lawyer, Hector Orley, had promised to investigate.

The previous year the courthouse in Sunrise had proved to be too small for its growing county so it had been torn down and a new one started. But the harsh winter had stalled construction, and Lassiter's trial was to be held in the Sunrise schoolhouse.

Because he was considered dangerous, Lassiter was taken from the county jail to the schoolhouse in a wagon with his wrists manacled and a two-foot spread of chain between his legs.

All heads in the jammed courtroom turned when Lassiter was marched down the aisle, chains clanking. There were a few smiles of encouragement, winks. But most viewed him with outrage, for he had committed cold-blooded murder and should pay for the crime.

Lassiter's lawyer, Hector Orley, gave him a brief nod. A tall, stoop-shouldered man with thinning sandy hair, Orley peered at his client through brass-framed spectacles and muttered "good morning," but his tone of voice indicated that there was little good in it. He specialized in mines and riparian rights, and had never practiced criminal law.

Lassiter looked around the crowded courtroom for Doc Maydon's white head, but failed to see him. He felt let down. But his spirits brightened when he caught sight of Victoria Reed. She seemed pale and drawn, but managed a bright smile.

"The witness against you," Orley said, nodding his head toward a young blond girl who sat tensely at a table where the county prosecutor overflowed into a chair. County Prosecutor Jeremiah Whick was a jolly, plump man. Telfont and Whick exchanged spare smiles, and Lassiter's wound began to throb slightly.

Judge Oscar Peabody came bounding in from a side room, a dapper little man in a freshly ironed brown suit, his hair on his small skull slick with pomade. He pulled out a large gold watch and looked directly at the prosecutor and lawyer for the defense.

"Gents, I've got another case to try this afternoon. So let's not dally." He crashed down his gavel. "Court's in session."

Jeremiah Whick stood, cleared his throat pompously, and began his opening statement to the jury of a dozen stern-faced males. He stated that Lassiter had lured Betain out of town, hoping to rob him of the remaining funds left over from the railroad.

When a raging Lassiter leaped to his feet, yelling that it was a lie, the judge ordered him to sit down. Sheriff Ian McKenzie caught him by the arm and jerked him back to his chair, where he sat fuming and listening to the rest of it.

"All lies," he hissed to Orley at his side. But the lawyer did not respond. He was slumped in his chair, doodling on a piece of paper with a yellow pencil.

Whick called the witness for the prosecution. Wilbur Dover gave the ashen-faced Ivy Eading a reassuring pat on the arm. She walked woodenly to the witness chair and was sworn in. She presented a picture of propriety in her prim brown dress with her blond hair slicked back and knotted at the back of her neck.

After clearing her throat, she answered Whick's questions. Yes, she had witnessed the defendant draw a gun and murder Corse Betain. At Whick's insistence, she leveled a trembling forefinger. "Lassiter is the man," she said in such hushed tones the judge ordered her to repeat it.

Hector Orley made a lame attempt at cross examination, but the Eading girl did not change her story. She had been no more than twenty feet away, on a morning ride out of town to enjoy the beautiful mountain scenery. She had gone further than intended, and as she was about to turn back, she had heard angry voices. That was when she had followed the sound and witnessed the tragedy. Yes, Betain had managed to get off one lucky shot that had wounded Lassiter, but that was when he was dying.

Spectators leaned forward breathlessly so as not to miss a word. On the wall the clock in its varnished case ticked away the minutes.

Jeremiah Whick turned to Lassiter's lawyer and said with a smile, "Well, looks like that's about it, Hector." And when Hector Orley nodded his head, an outraged Lassiter seized him by the arm.

"You're not through yet by a damn sight," he hissed.

"Do you have a witness to refute the young lady's testimony?"

Before Lassiter could reply, Victoria Reed jumped to her feet and demanded to be heard. In the pandemonium that followed, with the judge pounding his gavel and everyone talking, Victoria's voice was drowned out. Finally everyone calmed down, and she was allowed to speak.

"I want to be called as a witness!" she said in a

loud, firm voice. "To let everyone know what a horrible person Corse Betain really was."

"How would you know?" Jeremiah Whick demanded, coming out of his chair.

"The whole valley knows how he stole money—"

"Made foolish financial moves, perhaps," Whick interrupted smoothly. "But still he was a human being and he is dead. Dead at the hands of the man known as Lassiter." He pointed dramatically at the accused, who sat stiffly, his mouth a grim line across his dark face.

"I knew Corse Betain better than anyone!" Victoria cried, her voice breaking.

"How is that?" Whick demanded

"Because I am his *widow!*"

Whick's mouth dropped open as gasps swept the courtroom and every head turned to the tall girl with the squarish face, thick brows, her red-gold hair flaming in the sunlight and her eyes blazing defiance.

"You mean to say you were married to the late Mr. Betain?" the judge demanded.

"Yes!"

Whick allowed a plump tongue to race across his lower lip. Then he recovered from his surprise and said to Victoria, who seemed to be fighting tears, "Such a marriage as you speak of is certainly not common knowledge."

"He . . . he wanted to keep it a secret. For the present—"

"So that accounts for the gossip." Whick smiled and spread his pudgy hands.

"Yes, the gossip because he stayed all night at my place. Many times."

"Just where were you married, may I ask?"

"At Juniper. It is a matter of record at the Aspen County Courthouse."

"We shall see . . ." Whick said.

"Lassiter didn't murder my husband!" Victoria cried, her voice breaking. "I know he didn't."

"You have proof?" Whick shot back.

"He told me he didn't. And . . . and I believe him."

Everyone began talking at once. Judge Peabody banged his gavel, looked narrowly at his large gold watch, then snapped the case shut.

"I think we've heard enough." He scowled at the jury. "Have you?"

Twelve heads nodded.

Lassiter was on his feet again. "Wait a minute!" McKenzie yanked him back to his chair.

The jurors were leaning toward each other to converse in hushed tones. Everyone looked on in breathless silence. The clock on the wall bonged the hour.

The judge asked impatiently if they had reached a verdict. The foreman got to his feet. "Guilty," he said tonelessly, looking directly at Lassiter. Lassiter sat in stunned silence.

"Well, in that case," the judge said in a loud voice, "I have no choice but to sentence you, Lassiter, to hang by the neck until you are dead." He banged his gavel and got to his feet. Victoria Reed screamed and Ivy Eading looked as if she might faint.

Then the little judge wheeled around and said as an afterthought, "And may God have mercy on your soul. By the way, the execution is set for Wednesday morning at nine A.M. And I suggest that children be closely confined to the schoolhouse so they can't sneak away and witness the . . . er . . . proceedings."

Peabody came around the teacher's desk and shook Jeremiah Whick by the hand. "I thank you for speeding up this grisly business so it didn't drag on into the afternoon. You, too," he added to Lassiter's lawyer. And to Lassiter, who sat rigidly with a frown on his face, "Sorry you're gonna die. But we got to have law an' order."

Then he went skipping up the aisle, pushing his way through the crowd. Lassiter noticed bitterly that many reached out to slap him on the arm or the back. Most of the spectators, especially those who had driven in from the far corners of the county, looked satisfied. No hitch had developed and they were going to get their entertainment after all. In a way, seeing Lassiter hang would make up for their frustrations concerning the Sunrise Valley Railroad Company.

Lassiter's eyes found Victoria Reed's in the throng. She lifted a trembling hand, tried to smile encouragement. As she started toward him, Sheriff McKenzie marched Lassiter out a side door, relocked his wrists in manacles and put him in the wagon for the trip back to the county jail.

All up and down the street those citizens who had been unable to crowd into the schoolhouse watched somberly as the sheriff's wagon, driven by a lank deputy named Durkin, proceeded through the sudden tangle of traffic.

"Jesus Christ, Wednesday mawnin'," McKenzie complained to Dirk Foley who was riding beside the wagon, a sawed-off shotgun across his thigh. "Damn judge don't realize all the work that's gotta be done in one day. Got to get word to Curt Bascom that he's got another twenty bucks comin' as hangman. Then see that the damn gallows is workin' properly. Last time you remember, the trap door stuck an' we had a helluva time gettin' that poor bastard hung."

Lassiter, hunched in the bed, allowed his body to sway with the rhythm of the wagon as it clattered over ruts and stones. In order to avoid the belligerent stares of the crowd lining the street, he looked beyond the town at the granite peaks touched by sunlight and scarred from centuries of erosion. They were peaceful looking, but they could be killers just as surely as the skeleton structure in the weedgrown lot behind the jail. Lassiter took a final look at the mountains, wondering if after Wednesday he would ever see them again. Then he forcibly put such an idea from his mind. Somehow he would extricate himself from this quagmire.

That little blond bitch was the one who had put him in this predicament. But how to get her to change her story?

The wagon came to a halt beside the unpainted gallows with the thirteen steps. The trap door hung down, stirring slightly in the faint breeze.

When Lassiter was again locked in the cell, manacles removed and ankles freed, Sheriff McKenzie said through the barred door, "Reckon you can order anythin' to eat that strikes your fancy."

"A pie with a cell door key baked in it would suit me fine."

McKenzie laughed and slapped his thigh. "I like that. You can still joke about things. It'll make the business Wednesday a lot easier for all of us if you can keep a smile on your face."

Lassiter's smile was hard enough to cut through glass. The sheriff failed to notice.

Lassiter worried that Doc Maydon hadn't appeared at the trial. What had kept him away? Later that day he asked McKenzie about it, but the sheriff waved his hands and said he was too busy to think much about it. Only that he had heard Doc had gone out of town yesterday to see a patient.

"Then why didn't he come back?" Lassiter shouted through the bars, but McKenzie had walked away. The office door slammed.

Several times on the long ride to Aspen Ridge, Doc Maydon had been on the point of turning back. Damn it, he didn't want to miss the trial tomorrow and if the Strothers woman had a protracted labor it might happen. But each time the idea crossed his mind, he thrust it aside in favor of the Hippocratic Oath.

By the time he arrived at the isolated Strothers place, it was raining heavily in the high mountains—and he learned that the wife wasn't even pregnant.

Strothers and his frail wife were mighty surprised to see the doctor. Because he was tired and it was raining hard, the doctor accepted their invitation to stay over night. He got little sleep in the house that smelled of stale grease and food. But he was eager to start out early the following morning in the bright sunshine.

Doc was thinking about Lassiter's trial when he came around the bend in the road and caught sight of a stealthy movement in the pines up ahead. Cold sweat suddenly bathed his back.

"Damn it, I knew from the first I shouldn't have come," he said aloud to himself and made a clumsy grab for the revolver under his coat. But on the muddy road his fumbling draw produced a tongue of flame from the shadowed trees. The shot knocked him backward off the rump of his horse and onto the road. As the sky pinwheeled overhead, he somehow sat up and finished his draw. He failed to feel or hear the second shot for it struck him in the center of the forehead.

Red-haired Shanley and the towering Ream stepped from the trees and looked him over. Then they dragged the body to one side of the road.

"Likely be some days before he's found," Shanley said. "An' by then there won't be much left after the coyotes git through."

Both men smiled and rode toward Sunrise.

CHAPTER EIGHTEEN

When Ivy finished waiting on a complaining woman who had bought yards of calico, Wilbur Dover hissed in her ear, "Thursday, the day after the hangin', my wife's takin' the stage to Denver."

"I . . . I think I'll be leaving, Mr. Dover."

For a moment the little man looked crushed, then he thrust out his chest and said, "You can't leave. I need you to help run the store with my wife away. Besides," he added craftily, "You don't get paid 'less you stay out the whole month. Thirty-two round silver dollars you got comin'. He touched her arm, its smooth warmth causing his heart to nearly burst from his chest. "Plus a bonus, Ivy. A *bonus!*"

She thought of her own meager funds, hardly enough to see her all the way back to Tucson. Mostly that afternoon her mind was filled with the trial and Lassiter. She thought back to the day she had followed him and Betain out of town, tried to remember what she had overheard.

She remembered Lassiter telling Betain that he

and Xavier Betain had been waylaid by a pair of cut-throats. Cutthroats, he had called Charlie and Chick.

"You mentioned money," Betain had said that day.

"Your father sent it with me. I'm to get two thousand dollars for my trouble."

"You have something in writing?"

"I expected your pa to be alive when it was over."

"Well then, it seems you might not have a leg to stand on, Lassiter."

There had been harsh words. Then, peeking through the trees, Ivy saw to her surprise that Betain had drawn a gun and was pointing it at Lassiter.

"Thanks for telling me exactly where you buried the money, Lassiter. And for that, all you get is *adios*."

More talk, more swearing and then a gunshot that made Ivy jump. A glance showed her that Lassiter was down. She turned to flee in panic as another gunshot erupted, rattling through the trees.

Suddenly she saw Telfont and three other horsemen veering in from the road. Terrified, she hid in the trees, but from the corner of her eye she saw Betain, limping, come to a halt not twenty feet from where she was hidden.

She heard yelling from Telfont and the others. Then the next thing she knew Telfont was plunging after Betain. Both Telfont and Gilbey hovered over Betain who was lying on the ground. He still gripped a revolver, and with a snarl he turned it on Telfont. Telfont shot him dead.

She finally reached her horse and spurred toward Sunrise, but Jud Ream came after her and brought her back.

And from that moment on, terror had lodged in her heart like a cold stone.

Ever since the trial, Lassiter's face had floated in and out of her consciousness. She had to see that face once again in person, to rekindle her rage at Charlie's death and the need for vengeance—and to justify the lies she had told.

She, who hated liars and thieves above all else. She gave a sorry little laugh and then angrily wiped away the tears that threatened to dampen the front of her brown dress.

Just before sundown she slipped away from the store and went over to the jail. In the alley she saw several men at a cell window and knew it was Lassiter's from the names they were calling him.

She had hoped to see him alone. As she hesitated, the men drifted away one by one, and headed home for supper.

When she was finally alone, she walked over to the window. The warning signed by Sheriff McKenzie had been torn down. She lifted a corner of the heavy canvas and peered into the cell. It was long and narrow and had a cot, a table, and a chair. Lassiter was pacing the cell on his long legs, hands clasped behind his back, head down as if in deep thought. As he neared the window, he looked up and saw her. Something flickered across his mouth and deep into his eyes so that they glittered.

She stepped back from the bars, afraid he might reach through and try to throttle her. She looked up and saw him in the window, the rage gone from his dark face. There was nothing there to read.

"Did you come to gloat?" he asked in a low, tense voice.

"Maybe, in a way." She looked at him defiantly, churning up all her old anger.

"I thought it was something like that. But why?"

"You killed Charlie Baxter."

At first the name meant nothing, but then, looking into the sweet young face that was trying to look so hard, he seized on the first name. "You mean *Charlie!*"

Hearing the name caused tears to spring to her eyes. "You murdered him." Her voice was shaking so he could barely hear her. By now the shadows were lengthening along the alley and through the poplars he could see a window blossom suddenly with lamplight.

"I didn't murder him."

"You shot him down and to me it's the same thing."

"You must have been there that day to know about it."

"I was. I saw most of it—"

"Then you rode away. You were the third member of the outfit. I'll be damned. A girl."

"Now Charlie's been avenged," she said tremulously and started to turn away.

"Wait. I didn't kill him. Betain's father did. Your friend Charlie and the other one had me whipsawed. This Charlie of yours was gunned down by the old man. A lucky rifle shot or I wouldn't be here today." And, thinking of the coming Wednesday, he added to himself, *Maybe it's too bad that I am.* Then he angrily stepped on the gloomy thought.

She stood rigid, one hand pressed to her cheek, her eyes downcast as if counting the ruts and hoof and bootprints on the alley floor.

"You didn't see that part of it," Lassiter went on quietly. "If you had, you'd have known the truth."

She was silent for several moments, then slowly she lifted her head. Her small teeth were sunk deep in her lower lip, and anguish was heavy in her eyes. "When I heard the shooting that day I ran to my horse and got away. I was scared out of my wits—"

"Will you tell the truth now about me and Corse Betain?"

But she had turned and was running away.

He made such a clamor at the cell door that finally McKenzie, swearing, came to see what it was all about.

Lassiter told him about the girl and what she had said, McKenzie staring at him skeptically through the bars. "I was almost beginning to have some halfway respect for you, Lassiter, but you tryin' to make out that the little lady is a per ... per ... perjurer, I guess it is ... well, it's just too goddamn much."

He slammed his way back to the office.

All Monday night the guilty verdict rang in Lassiter's mind like cathedral bells. He only managed snatches of sleep. In the morning he again tried to get the sheriff to listen to him, but a stone-faced McKenzie refused.

Lassiter was forced to submit to a further indignity. A heavy chain was looped around his waist and fastened with a large padlock. The other end of the chain was padlocked to an iron ring embedded in the wall midway between the door and the window so he couldn't reach either one. Sheriff McKenzie had sensed the burgeoning desperation of his prisoner and was taking no chances.

The keys to the padlocks, Lassiter noted, were on a separate iron ring too large to be slipped into a pocket.

To be hampered in his movements by a chain was something he hadn't counted on. His mind had been filled with plans for a jail break. He was remembering one time when he had been held in a jail cell down at Costa Sur on a trumped-up charge. He had escaped. Somehow he would duplicate the feat here in Sunrise. He ground his teeth together and tried to figure out a way to make it work.

Somehow he would survive. He had to. There was too much living left to do to end it here in Sunrise, jerking his life away at the end of a rope.

From the yard came a squeal of hinges as the hangman readied the gallows for operation. There was much joshing back and forth between the man and the onlookers.

Finally the hangman, chubby and jovial, came to stand at the cell door to try and evaluate Lassiter's weight. "About one eighty-five, I'd say. That right, mister?"

Lassiter only glared at the man.

"No sense bein' bitter about it," said the hangman through the bars of the cell door. He seemed affronted. "Last winter when I hung Bernie Peoples me an' him joshed right up to the minute I put the black cap over his head. An' the last thing I heard was him laughin'. I tell you, he went out like a gentleman, not like the scowlin' bear you seem to be."

Jerking his bowler hat low over his eyes, he stalked away, boots ringing in the corridor. Later Lassiter heard a great thumping sound from the yard and guessed it was a canvas bag filled with enough sand to make it weigh one eighty-five. He smiled grimly to himself.

Twice that afternoon Victoria Reed tried to get in to see him. The office door was open so he could hear her voice. But both times McKenzie refused, saying, "I can let you see him five minutes while he's havin' breakfast in the mornin'."

Because a crowd had started to gather outside Lassiter's window, McKenzie ordered Dirk Foley to parade up and down the alley with his sawed-off shotgun. Townspeople and visitors soon got the idea and stayed away from Foley's grinning horse-teeth and his Greener.

Lassiter's mind churned with ideas of escape. But as quickly as they popped into his head, they were discarded. A cold sweat of desperation began to dampen his body. But still he refused to believe that tomorrow meant the end of everything. By God, *no!*

Just after sundown Lordine Maxwell herself brought his supper from her cafe because she had never been around a condemned man before and thought the experience would be exciting. She entered his cell, wearing a broad smile, the fatty parts of her bouncing. But she was careful to keep out of his reach, beyond the end of his chain. She set the tray on the table that had been dragged near the door and out of Lassiter's reach.

When he saw her approach, Lassiter built a hope that in some way he might use her corpulent body as a shield. But even as he thought about it he realized he could never bring himself to risk the life of a female in such a daring venture.

"Best food there is from my place," she beamed.

Then she pushed the table up within his reach and scampered out.

Dirk Foley, shotgun under his arm, locked the cell door.

Lordine Maxwell lingered, her plump face pressed against the bars. "Eat hearty, 'cause you only get one more meal. I'm s'posed to bring breakfast afore seven o'clock. 'Cause you'll be gone by eight."

Hearing her say it in such a jovial way caused a cold shudder to race down Lassiter's backbone.

The food was tasty. He had no appetite, but he forced himself to eat because a long night stretched ahead of him. Already he had made up his mind that sometime during that long night he was going to get out of this place.

Telfont appeared shortly after eight o'clock. Dirk Foley, who had been sitting in a tipped-back chair in the corridor, shotgun across his lap, listened to something Telfont whispered and then went into the office and closed the door.

Telfont came over to Lassiter's cell. "Time's running out on you, Lassiter. You feel like talking about the . . ." he looked both ways along the corridor then said, ". . . the money?"

Lassiter shook his head. Only minutes before he had seen a harmless large brown bug climb through his window from the alley and drop clumsily to the cell floor. It offered a way . . . a mighty slim chance . . . of making his escape.

Telfont spoke in a low voice charged with emotion. "You've got less than twelve hours of life ahead. Draw me a map and I'll see that you're out of here."

Lassiter laughed. Telfont's face tightened.

"All right, I'll get you out of here first. We'll go together and dig up the money. Then you can be on your way."

"With a bullet in the back of the head," Lassiter said with a hard grin.

"No, nothing like that. I'm trying to do you a favor."

"Listen Telfont, I've made my peace with the Lord and I'm resigned to my fate."

Telfont stared at him incredulously, then a smile flickered across his lips under the waxed mustache. "Not you, Lassiter. Hell, no. You're resigned in a pig's eye."

"Believe me, I know when my string's run out."

Sheriff McKenzie opened the office door and leaned into the corridor. "Kee-ryst, Marcus," he said softly, "I can't let you stay in there for the rest of the night."

"Coming," Telfont said, casting an ugly look in Lassiter's direction.

After Telfont had gone, Lassiter heard McKenzie say to his deputy, "Dirk, I'm kinda worried an' I figure you an' me oughta not leave Lassiter to nobody else but us. It's his last night an' I don't trust nobody else."

"I'll take first watch," Dirk Foley said with a tense smile.

"Naw, we'll flip for it."

"I got a coin. Heads I git first watch, tails you do. All right, Sheriff?"

"Toss the coin."

"Be damned," Foley said with a shake of his head. "It's come up heads."

When the sheriff had left, Foley moved a heavy chair closer to Lassiter's cell. He hung the keys to the padlock and the cell door on a hook above his tipped-back chair.

"Just in case we have a fire or somethin'," Foley said, showing his oversized teeth. "Wouldn't want you to burn to a crisp or nothin' like that."

Still grinning, he pulled the shotgun onto his lap. But he didn't seem to be able to settle down. He was on edge and prowled the corridor, opening the office door and peering into it as if waiting for someone to come or something to happen.

Lassiter wondered why the deputy seemed so nervous. Lassiter didn't know there was a plan to break him out of jail. It was to be done by three men wearing black hoods.

After his last words with Lassiter, Telfont had grown increasingly anxious. Lassiter wasn't budging about the money and he was due to hang at eight o'clock in the morning.

Telfont was in Teeley's brooding about it when the idea came to him. He recalled Etta Dempster remarking once that her housekeeper-maid, Fiona, was a great seamstress.

His mind boiling with plans, he downed his drink and walked through the trees to the Dempster house at the edge of town. Lamplight glowed on the lower floor and thin Fiona in her starched uniform opened the door; she hadn't as yet gone home.

Etta came downstairs at her call, looking angry. "I was just getting ready for bed," she complained.

"So early? A beautiful woman like you?"

"Oh, stop it, Marcus." She came down to the entry

hall where he was standing. Fiona had gone into the back part of the house, getting ready to depart for her quarters.

Telfont came up to her and had his arms around her lush figure before she could fend him off.

"You never come around unless you want something," she snapped, her black eyes large and accusing.

"And I do want something tonight," he said with a debonair smile. He kissed her cheek, moved to her mouth, and was rewarded when her breasts rose and fell with quickening breath.

Finally he pulled away from her. "You remember the money you said Corse Betain's father was sending?"

"I'm convinced it was one of Corse's pipe dreams. . . ." Then her eyes narrowed. "Why are you bringing it up?"

"The money actually came."

She gasped. "Then where is it?"

"Lassiter buried it."

"Lassiter!"

Telfont smiled to himself because he knew her mind was spinning. He knew her so well. At one time or another she had obviously had Lassiter within reach but had failed to capitalize on it.

"There's a lot of money involved, Etta. I haven't said anything before because I wasn't sure. Not until now."

"Your little peasant told you, I suppose."

"I finally got it out of her. Somehow Lassiter has got to be reached."

"Maybe I could do it," she said, her rich voice rising in excitement.

He shook his head. "It's too late for that. No, I've got things fixed with Dirk Foley. But I need your help."

She stepped back, her beautiful face suddenly hard. "So that's why you came. You *do* want something."

He pulled her into his arms again and began raining kisses on her face until she was fighting for breath. "Yes, as you can see there is something I want." He looked down into her face. "But something else of equal importance."

"Such as?"

"You told me once that Fiona is an expert with a needle."

"She is, but I don't understand—"

"I want her to make three hoods. For three large men."

"Hoods?"

"To go over the head. If we hurry, you can get to the Dover Store before it closes. They're open late tonight because of all the people who've come in for the hanging tomorrow. I want you to buy enough black cloth for the hoods. Say it's for a dress."

"And what will all this do for . . . us?"

"The money, Etta. Lassiter will be pulled out of that jail. In a safe place he'll be made to talk. Then the money . . . is ours."

"It does sound exciting."

"Come on, we don't have any time to lose."

"I'll have to take the buggy, I can't possibly walk that far."

"The hell you can't, my dear. We won't waste time hitching up a buggy. And by the way, tell Fiona to wait for us to come back."

"Can we trust Fiona not to talk?"

"If she has a conscience, money will cool it down. If not . . . there are other means." His voice had hardened.

"You mean—"

"No, nothing like that," he assured her with a smile. "I'll just put the fear of God in her. It's been known to work." He laughed.

"At times you are a demon, Marcus," she said, her teeth shining.

As he walked her rapidly toward the center of town he thought of his plans. Gilbey, Ream and Shanley were agreeable to the jail break. Especially after being assured that Dirk Foley was in on it and would offer no resistance. He had promised each of them five thousand dollars. He rather liked Gilbey, but the other two . . . well, there were ways of saving himself ten thousand dollars.

With the Betain money and what he already had hidden away in a bank in another county, he was set. If he decided to stay in Sunrise he'd have to make some provision for Etta Dempster, he supposed. Moving in with the lady would probably solve the problem, he thought with smug satisfaction.

CHAPTER NINETEEN

It was a little past ten o'clock Lassiter guessed. A stiff wind caused the canvas window cover to flap against the bars. He glanced at Dirk Foley, who was dozing in his tipped-back chair under the corridor bracket lamp that had been turned low.

Taking a deep breath, Lassiter yelled, "Hey, what in the hell!" and rattled his chain.

Foley came abruptly awake, the legs of his chair slamming against the plank floor. "Wha . . . wha . . . what's the matter?" he managed to get out.

"*Scorpion!*"

Foley gave a snort, looking disgusted. "What about it?"

"Damn thing came in the window. Biggest one I ever saw." Lassiter made his voice shake.

"The hell with it," Foley muttered sleepily.

"We both drop off to sleep it might get on me. Or *you!*"

Foley rubbed sleep from his eyes, glanced along the deserted corridor and got to his feet. He came over to the cell door and peered in. "Where's it at, the scorpion?"

"Under the bed, near the wall."

"Stomp it."

"Not me," Lassiter protested. "Down in Mexico the natives claim a big one like that will jump at a man. Sting him to death before he can blink."

"This ain't Mexico."

"This one's got a stinger bigger than this." Lassiter crooked the index finger of his right hand to illustrate the point. Foley looked at it and rubbed his jaw. Then, looking disgusted but at the same time wary, he unlocked the door.

"Face the wall," he ordered. "You make one wrong move an' you'll have a double dose of buckshot up your ass."

"All I care about is you killing that scorpion. . . ." Lassiter faced the wall as ordered.

Foley crept into the cell and went to the foot of the bed. Bending down, he gingerly pulled aside the bed clothes that touched the floor. He was staring at the large brown bug that had been partially flattened under Lassiter's boot.

"I see the damn thing!" Foley shouted.

Lassiter moved with such blinding speed that Foley only had time to look around before Lassiter's knuckles crashed into the point of Foley's jaw. As Foley opened his mouth to yell, Lassiter clubbed him with both fists, tore the shotgun from his grasp and threw it on the bed. Then he gripped Foley's thick neck in both hands and started to exert pressure. When he reached the point where Foley was writhing and gasping, turning red, his eyes bulging, Lassiter eased off.

"Here's what you're going to do, Foley," Lassiter hissed. "You're going out in that hall and bring back the keys to this padlock. And every inch of the way the twin barrels of this shotgun will be on you."

Foley was on his knees. The redness had receded and his face had turned ashen. He eyed the shotgun in Lassiter's hands and licked his lips. "You can't never git away with this—"

"I'm going to, Foley. I haven't got one damn thing to lose by killing you. The rope can go around my neck only once!"

"It . . . it's crazy—"

"And don't count on the cell bars blocking some of the buckshot. Enough will get through to cut you to pieces. And you know it. You stand right in the cell door where I can watch you. And if you try and run to put the wall between you and me, you won't make it. You'll be dead. Splattered all over the wall."

Holding the shotgun in one hand, Lassiter reached out for Foley's belt gun and shoved it into his waistband.

"Now you march, Foley. *March!*"

Foley, still dazed from the blow to his jaw and the later clubbing, moved almost drunkenly toward the corridor. Lassiter could tell from his jerky steps that he was halfway tempted to make a break for it. Facing any other weapon but a sawed-off shotgun, Foley might have attempted to run. But the lethal barrels of the weapon could literally cut a man in two at this close range. Clearly Foley wasn't about to risk being torn to pieces by a scythe of buckshot. He was already unhooking the ring of keys and stepping back into the cell. "Now unlock the padlock at my waist," Lassiter ordered. "And if you even take a deep breath, I'll blow a hole in you big enough for a full-sized calf."

The lock clicked in Foley's trembling hands. Lassiter pulled the padlock out of the links and threw it on the bed. When Foley was stepping back, Lassiter suddenly lunged. Reversing the shotgun, he slammed the butt end solidly against Foley's chin. The deputy collapsed to the floor and lay still. Lassiter took a few desperate moments to loop the chain around Foley's wrists and padlock it in place.

With his ears straining for any foreign sound, Lassiter ripped a strip from one of the blankets and used it to gag Foley.

Then, creeping to the hallway, he blew out the bracket lamp. With a taut feeling in his gut so strong it ached, Lassiter tiptoed along the corridor. He pressed his ear against the jail office door, but as near as he could tell there was no one in the office, only a meager show of lamplight under the door. Of course there'd be a night light in the sheriff's office. He scrubbed a forearm across his sweating brow and decided not to risk leaving by the front door. His heart seemed to boom in his chest as he moved toward the alley door. It was thick and studded with brass and locked on the inside with two heavy bolts twice the size of a man's thumb. When he worked the first one out there was a faint screech of metal on metal. He halted and held his breath, waiting. But there were no sounds to indicate anyone was coming to investigate. Taking a deep breath, he worked out the lower bolt and was just about to open the door when McKenzie stepped in from the office.

"Hey, Dirk, I just got word over at Teeley's that Doc Maydon was found shot to death . . . What the hell. What you doin' settin' in the dark? Hey, Dirk . . ."

McKenzie was starting to turn back for the office and a lamp when Lassiter got in behind him. "You've been fairly decent to me, Sheriff," he said, ramming the shotgun against his tailbone, "so don't make me kill you."

"Lassiter!" McKenzie turned his bearded face to stare over his shoulder in surprise.

"Keep your voice down." Lassiter pulled him away from the doorway where lamplight spilled.

"What're you gonna do—" It ended in a groan as Lassiter struck the sheriff on the back of the head with the twin barrels of the shotgun. As McKenzie's knees collapsed, Lassiter eased him down to the floor. Quickly putting aside the shotgun, he peeled off the sheriff's coat, then his shirt. He tore the shirt into strips, using these to bind wrists, ankles, and to provide a gag. Then, taking the sheriff's gun, he jammed it into the waistband of his trousers beside the one he'd appropriated from Foley. He picked up the shotgun and stepped back.

"Sorry, Sheriff," he muttered to the inert bundle crumpled on the floor.

Lassiter stepped out into the dark alley. Faint sounds of revelry drifted from Teeley's, celebrating in advance the hangman's production scheduled for the morning, he supposed.

He closed the alley door. He was breathing hard, every nerve in his body screaming with tension as he ran, hunched over, toward Teeley's nearly two blocks away. He kept his eyes open for a saddle horse, but saw none until he reached the front of the saloon.

The end horse was a pinto. As he vaulted into the saddle, he froze. Half a dozen men broke from the saloon and began running toward the livery barn in the trees a half a block away.

With a dry mouth, Lassiter reined the pinto away from the hitching post, expecting any moment for someone to yell, "That's my hoss!"

Lassiter was moving the pinto down the dark street at a walk when three other men burst from the saloon to race after the original group.

One of them was shouting to the hostler, "Hey, Willie! Git up, git up! We need hosses. Us an' the sheriff is gonna find who kilt Doc . . ."

They were almost at the stable door, shadowy figures in the trees moving at a trot. But then from the direction of the jail came two other dim figures and more shouting.

"Sheriff's out of it! So's Foley! Lassiter's gone! *Busted jail!*"

"Whaddaya mean, busted jail?" one of the men demanded in a dumbfounded voice.

"Escaped!" This from a panting man who barely got it out.

Knowing it was his only chance, and that very slim, Lassiter dug in his heels before he was spotted. The pinto fairly leaped down the moon-swept street.

"By kee-ryst, there he goes!" a man yelled, and punctuated his words with a blob of yellow-red flame from the muzzle of a gun. Something slammed into the wagonyard fence Lassiter was passing. Then he was bent over in the saddle, veering toward the thick trees on the far side of the stable. More bright flashes of gun muzzles sought him out.

But he reached the east end of town safely and was out into the flats beyond, the only sounds in his ears the thud of his wildly pumping heart and the hoofbeat of the hard-running pinto. For the moment at least, he had slipped from danger by the slimmest of margins. But for how long?

When at last he stopped at the foot of a low range of hills to let the horse blow, he could hear the faint sounds of thundering pursuit. As he stood beside his sweated horse, the enormity of the news he had heard began to sink in. Doc Maydon was dead, evidently murdered. His last friend in the town of Sunrise. Despair hit him like a dark shroud. Shaking his head, he mentally clawed his way out of it and started riding again.

His intention was to swing north for a few miles, then west into the higher mountains as he had done before. With any luck he'd be able to stop by the Plato Mine. There he would give Victoria Reed a map showing the location of the buried gold; it was hers by rights as she was Corse Betain's widow. Money to do with as she pleased. Someday she could send him the two thousand dollars he had coming, send it to some hideout he would choose deep in Mexico where Sunrise law couldn't reach him. It was up to her whether or not she fulfilled Xavier Betain's obligation.

All this was flashing through his mind as he got every possible measure of speed out of the pinto. Wind stung his eyes, and the stars glittered as the wind blew a bank of clouds over the mountains and allowed the moon to bathe the dark earth in its yellow glow.

Here the terrain was unknown to him and he had

to rely on sheer instinct. Soon he had to force the pinto through a stretch of thick brush. At the far end, at the shoulder of a hill, he let the animal blow again. He was doubling back in the general direction of Sunrise, but to the north, when the pinto began to limp badly. Lassiter groaned. *What now?* was the black thought that knifed through his mind.

Dismounting, he found that the pinto's right foreleg had been deeply cut, whether from a sharp-edged rock or a jutting branch of snapped-off brush, he couldn't tell. But whatever had caused the deep wound, the pinto was unfit for more hard riding.

In those few moments, with his throat tight, the palms of his hands clammy with sweat, he tried to judge just how far he had come from town. Far off through the trees he could see a faint haze of yellowed lights against a sky that had clouded over again. Suddenly it came to him that the only option was to corner Telfont and force the truth out of him. But he was at a loss to know just how to go about it.

The sounds of pursuit had faded and stopped altogether. He halted, straining his ears, listening with hope. Then the sounds started up again, coming his way. He guessed they had momentarily lost his trail. One of them, probably an experienced tracker, had seen where he had swung north and then west, and now they were headed that way.

All his horse could manage now was a limping walk. Ahead was a spine of hills dotted with skeletal juniper that ran in the general direction of town. He moved on until he reached the far side of the hill, then turned left, heading back in the general direction of Sunrise. With luck the pursuers would pound on past because here the ground was fairly hard in contrast to the sandy soil he had been on before.

He drew the shotgun from where he had been carrying it in a saddle scabbard and rode with it across his thigh. He wouldn't use it against his pursuers because most were undoubtedly townsmen and not of the Telfont ilk. But he would remind them that he had the shotgun, if they came too close, and with luck they would be impressed. Maybe not. If it ended here, that's the way it would have to be. He had always sensed that one day his life would end violently; he had decided long ago he was not destined for an old man's death, with boots off and lying in a feather bed. He had always hoped that when the end did come it would be in a fair fight with a better man, not shot to rags by a posse who suspected him of a murder he didn't commit.

Perhaps they would not expect him to return to town. It was a gamble, the greatest of his life. His nerves pulled with tension as he heard them coming. But miracle of miracles, they swept past the turnoff and on into the deeper hills, away from the town, not toward it.

Later, when he paused to rest his horse, he saw that it was bleeding badly from the leg wound. He knew it could not keep going much farther. He made a decision. Ahead he could see the glow of night lights from the town, much nearer now.

He stripped off saddle and bridle. He turned the weary animal loose with a slap on its rump. It went only a few feet, then halted, head down. Lassiter's heart went out to it. It had been a good horse to get him out of town so fast. But now he had done all that was possible under the circumstances. To push it further would have been cruel.

Burdened by the two pistols shoved in his belt, he discarded the S & W he had taken from Foley and kept the newer Colt .45 that had belonged to Ian McKenzie.

Then he started walking. . . .

CHAPTER TWENTY

At each step the town lights seemed to recede by just that much. He kept doggedly on and soon he was on the outskirts of Sunrise. A dog began to bark and he thought of the night he had appropriated the brown horse for Betain. So much had happened since. Betain and his past that was a total blank, at least for a time. And later on only pretending. Then, without waiting for Lassiter to reveal the hiding place of the money his father had sent, Betain going crazy with greed and drawing a pistol. And Lassiter convicted of killing him and sentenced to hang. What a disappointment, he thought wryly, for all the ranchers and their families who had come in for the event.

If the odds didn't narrow in his favor, he reminded himself as he stumbled along more or less blindly in the darkness, they would have their celebration after all.

He finally reached Telfont's house, the "mansion" at the east edge of town.

Every window in the big two-story house this night was dark. He smiled to himself. Was Telfont inside? If not, he would have to return eventually. He crept toward the house, taking cover behind the outbuildings, a shed, a privy, and now, another fair-sized shed. As he was debating how best to get into the house, three riders came in from the west. Lassiter, crouching at the shed, watched them dismount. One of them ran lightly up the wide porch steps and knocked on the front door.

Finally the shadowed figure went back down to the porch steps. "He ain't home."

"Mebbe he's over at Teeley's. Let's go see...." Lassiter recognized Joe Gilbey's voice. At that moment the moon suddenly broke free of the clouds. Gilbey's voice trailed off. "Who's that yonderly?"

"Where?" Jud Ream demanded, standing up in the stirrups.

"By the shed there. He ducked, but I seen him."

By then Lassiter was sprinting over the soft ground and into the protection of the tall trees.

"There he goes!" Gilbey shouted.

The yelling aroused a man some fifty yards away in a small house. He threw up the window and cried, "Might be Lassiter! He's loose!"

"You could be right," Gilbey shouted. "Jud, you head over to the left. Me 'n Red will head to the right an' try to run him down...."

As Lassiter ran hard he cursed the strong moonlight. After a block, he could still hear the three men calling to one another. The strenuous run tore at his lungs. He looked wildly around. There was more shouting behind him. To his left, across a narrow alley, he saw the familiar outlines of the funeral establishment owned by Wilbur Dover and the rear of his general store.

With a final burst of speed, he reached the deep shadows at the end of the porch. A door to his right swung open and a girl said in a low voice, "What's happening, Mr. Dover?"

Lassiter could barely make out her figure. She was leaning out, peering in the direction of the yelling and the hoofbeats.

As she stared, two riders came pounding into the alley and met a third. They galloped away together.

As the girl straightened up and looked more closely, Lassiter sprang at her, clapped a hand over her soft mouth and shoved her back into the room. He closed the door at his back and turned the key.

Moonlight fell through the narrow window and she recognized him. "Lassiter," she said in hushed surprise, speaking around the hand held at her mouth. He saw her eyes widen in alarm.

"I won't hurt you," he whispered.

Gilbey and the other two came roaring back to the alley. Lassiter could hear the mutter of excited voices as other men joined them.

"I see somethin' over by the hotel!" It was Red Shanley's shout. "Might be *him!*"

And some of them ran toward the hotel.

Another man yelled, "Seen somethin' move over by the livery barn! My God, I'm already, it *did* move!"

More scampering footsteps, then the harsh voice of Joe Gilbey nearby. "I got me a hunch he's around here. Let's have a good look!"

The noise had awakened Wilbur Dover and from a corner of the curtained window, Lassiter saw him creeping downstairs. He wore an old jacket and trousers pulled on over his nightshirt. His wife whimpered at the top of the stairs.

There was a thump of boots on the narrow porch near the girl's room. Lassiter stood looking at Ivy and she at him. In her long flannel nightgown she seemed demure and unworldly, but long ago he had guessed otherwise about her.

There was a sudden banging on her door, then Wilbur Dover's protest. "You can't go in there. Miss Eading—"

"Shut up, Dover," Gilbey snarled. "You in there, open up!"

"Watch out for him," a man yelled from some distance. "He's got Foley's shotgun!"

When the hammering on the door was repeated, Lassiter assumed it was all over.

"Just . . . just a minute . . ." Ivy's voice was steady. Standing on tiptoe, she whispered in Lassiter's ear. "Get into bed. Bunch up the covers. . . ." She pointed.

Forcibly Lassiter shook off any misgivings he might have about her and fairly dived into the bed. He stretched out, the shotgun at his side. He pulled the covers over him and as she had advised, bunched them up.

Through a fold in the blankets he saw her unlock the door and open it a crack. Gilbey jerked it all the way open.

"Lassiter's busted jail. He in here?"

"Of course he isn't," snapped an indignant Wilbur Dover. "Miss Eading is a decent young lady. . . ."

Gilbey ignored him. Shoving the girl aside, he

strode into the room and stood looking around at the small table, two chairs, and bed.

A curtained-off corner of the room evidently used as a closet caught Gilbey's attention. With drawn gun he marched past the bed and jerked the curtain aside.

"Only some of my clothes," Ivy said.

"Yeah." He stood looking around again. Lassiter was thankful that the only light was from the moon and it was faint at that. If Gilbey lighted the lamp on the table, he was gone.

But Gilbey only grunted something and stood staring at Ivy in the center of the room.

She said calmly, "I'm cold. I'm going back to bed. Please close the door when you go out."

"I'm gonna see you later, sweetheart," he said under his breath and gave her cheek a pinch.

But she said nothing and slipped into the bed that was still warm from her body. Lassiter could feel her softly pressed against him.

At the doorway Gilbey said, "If you spot Lassiter, yell!"

"I will," she said, drawing the covers up to her neck.

By then the men in the alley had rushed away to continue their search for the fugitive. Lassiter whispered, "Thanks."

He felt her shudder; she was curled on her side, her back to him. But she made no response.

"I'm gonna find Telfont," he continued to whisper. My hunch is he had Doc Maydon murdered. Doc was my only friend in this damned town."

"Now you have another friend . . . me. I've been doing a lot of thinking about the wrong I did you."

"Your testimony at the trial."

When she nodded her head in agreement he could feel her soft hair brush against his throat.

"Telfont scared you into it?"

"Partly. Partly it was because of . . . of Charlie Baxter."

"So you told me when you came to my window."

"The more I think about it, the more I realize that Charlie was just like Telfont in a lot of ways. He'd use people."

Lassiter started to whisper into her ear when there came a soft knock on the door. It opened. A shadowy figure crept in. Ivy gasped, hopped out of bed.

Wilbur Dover's voice shook. "My wife's gone back to bed, my darling. This is the night . . . for us."

"No, no . . ." She hurried over and placed both hands on his chest. They were about the same height, the slim girl and the storekeeper. "I'm too tired tonight," she whispered. "Tomorrow. I promise, Mr. Dover . . . Wilbur."

There were more breathless expressions of love on Dover's part, more protests, warmly spoken, from the girl.

"Tomorrow, Wilbur, tomorrow . . ."

Finally she got him out of the room, closed the door and locked it.

Only then did Lassiter exhale a long-held breath. Her teeth were chattering when she got back into the bed.

"Lordy, that was close," she gasped.

"Very."

She turned her head to look at him lying beside her. "I want to go with you, Lassiter. Wherever you go."

"Impossible."

"To make up for everything I did to you . . ."

It suddenly occurred to him that he hadn't heard Dover's footsteps crossing the porch and on the stairs. He stiffened and placed a finger across her lips, indicating silence. But she misunderstood and seized his whole hand and pressed her warm mouth against the palm.

As he lay there rigid with tension, he finally heard the porch creak. The doorknob was turning. Then Dover's low voice laden with passion: "Ivy, I figure you got him in there with you."

She gasped, "Oh, no, not at all . . ." trying to make it sound as if she was drugged with sleep.

"I remember seein' the two legs of the bed a little bit off the floor. Like there was a heavy weight on the far side. It's done that before with two people in the bed."

"Oh, gawd," she whispered.

"I'll let him go," Dover continued in quavering tones, "won't say a word. If'n you leave your door unlocked for me. "Please, Ivy, please . . ."

Lassiter leaped over Ivy and in one bound was at the door, turning the key, flinging it open. A startled Wilbur Dover tried to duck, but Lassiter dragged him into the room by a hard hand at the front of his nightshirt.

Lassiter flung him onto the bed, shoved the twin bores of the shotgun into his anguished face.

"You keep shut or you're dead," he threatened.

From several blocks away came the sound of shouting, then the thunder of horses at a run. Lassiter stiffened. Then the riders were sweeping out of town, probably on another wild-goose chase. Or so he hoped.

He handed the shotgun to the girl. "Keep him covered."

Seizing the thinnest of the blankets, he ripped it into strips as he had done with the deputy's shirt. Then he bound Dover hand and foot and gagged him. Dover's terrified eyes stared up at him.

"Don't try and get loose till daylight. If you do, I'll come back and finish you."

He turned to Ivy. "Get your clothes on. You want to come with me, well all right. But you've got to keep out of the business I figure to finish first."

"Yes, yes," she whispered and threw off her nightdress.

In the faint light, the staring eyes of Dover nearly burst from his head as he got a glimpse of rounded white young flesh. Clothing quickly covered it.

She got Charlie's .45 and dropped it into the pocket of her short coat. The weight of it pulled the garment out of shape.

Then they slipped out into the chilly darkness. Lassiter locked the door, threw the key across the alley, then took Ivy's arm. Looking both ways along the alley and seeing no one, he ran with her into a thick stand of pines. He kept to the deepest shadows, heading in the direction of Telfont's ornate dwelling.

"After I beat that bastard down to his socks will you tell the truth about Betain? That I didn't kill him?"

She was short of breath as she tried to keep up with him. She realized that changing her story would probably earn her a prison cell. A chill rippled along her spine.

"It's the least I can do, Lassiter," she panted. "I nearly got you hung."

He looked around at the girl running at his side. How far could he trust her? he wondered. Well, first things first. Try to bring Telfont to his knees then go on from there. He knew the smart thing to do was cut loose from the girl, steal another horse and put miles between himself and Sunrise. But if he did that, Telfont would have won. And he couldn't let that happen. Among other things, he knew as sure as he knew the sun would rise in the east that Telfont was responsible for the murder of Doc Maydon. . . .

CHAPTER TWENTY-ONE

Telfont's place loomed up in the moon-swept night with all the majesty of an English castle. It sprawled in the middle of five acres of pine. Lassiter was gambling that Telfont would have to return home sometime. And he intended to be ready for him.

Lassiter was rewarded by a light glowing in the lower front of the house. But the rest of it, including the upstairs, was dark. Approaching warily, he saw three horses tethered in front, their manes and tails ruffled by the chill breeze.

As Lassiter halted in the trees, breathing hard, he saw a shadowed figure pass a side window. It looked as if it might be Telfont, but he couldn't be sure.

Lassiter was sure it was Telfont when he moved closer a few moments later. Telfont paraded back and forth before the front and side windows, hands clasped behind his back as if in deep thought.

From the far side of town came dim shouts, and the sounds of more horses at a hard run. But thankfully the sounds were diminishing.

Then Lassiter saw Gilbey's thick figure through the window. He was talking to Telfont. Lassiter crept closer until he could hear Telfont's loud voice. "And stay away until you find him. Lassiter's around here someplace. Find him and bring him here. Now get at it. I've got some work to do."

Telfont made waving motions toward the front door with his hands.

Gilbey, Jud Ream and Red Shanley stepped out, closing the heavy front door. Lassiter tensed, wondering if it might be a trick of some kind, but they clattered on down the wide veranda steps, vaulted into the saddle and galloped toward the center of town.

"You've got him alone, Lassiter," Ivy whispered. She stood so close to him he could feel her body tremble with excitement.

"I'm not so sure," was his low-voiced response.

He studied the shadows around the house, the outbuildings. He could still hear the sounds of the horses fading. Were there now as many hoofbeats as there were at first? he asked himself. Was he imagining things?

But one thing he knew for sure, he either had to make a move, and quickly, or get out of town before dawn.

With Ivy following him soundlessly, he started to make a complete circle of the great house. His hands sweated on the sawed-off shotgun. The Colt he had shoved in his waistband was a hard lump against his stomach. He halted now and then to listen.

At the rear of the house he heard a horse stomp the ground out by the shadowed barn. Lassiter moved that way, keeping to the cover of the trees. He found a saddled horse tied off behind the shed, a big Morgan. How long had it been here? he wondered. Then the truth ripped across his mind.

He got Ivy by the arm and drew her close enough to whisper in her ear. "It's a trick. There's two of 'em in the house. Telfont and one of the others."

"You sure?"

"But I've got to get Telfont. And end this damn business once and for all."

"I'm a good shot . . ."

He shook his head. "You stay out here. That's what I'm getting at. You hear me?" He gave her shoulder a slight shake to emphasize the warning.

She didn't say anything, but just looked up at him, her rounded eyes reflecting moonlight.

That should have alerted him, but he was too keyed up to ponder it. He crept toward the rear of the house, shotgun at the ready. He tried the back door. It was locked. Then, heart pounding, he cautiously climbed the rear stairs leading to the veranda. For several feet he tiptoed along the veranda until he finally reached the window that gave off a faint glow of lamplight. Peering in he glimpsed Telfont, through several open doorways, in the front room bent over a desk. He was writing on a sheet of paper, pausing to dip his pen in the inkwell. By straining his ears, Lassiter could hear the faint scratch of pen on paper. Lassiter stared at the bent head, seeing the black hair that curled down Telfont's neck, the broad shoulders in the dark coat.

Gingerly he reached out for the window, exerted

pressure and found it to be unlocked. He withdrew his hand, thinking, too easy. Too damned easy. Yet his only chance lay in getting a confession out of Telfont.

Drawing a deep breath, Lassiter slid the window all the way up. It was noiseless, not even a rattle of glass. Count your blessings, Lassiter, he reminded himself.

Just as quietly, Lassiter closed the window so Telfont wouldn't be alerted by a fresh blast of cold night air.

He found he was in a library with a faint odor of leather from book bindings and chairs. The walls were lined with books. There was an unlighted fireplace and a large desk. He wondered why Telfont hadn't chosen this room to do his scribbling; a logical choice instead of the parlor. Part of the trap, of course. He could fairly smell it.

But there was no backing out now. The guilty one was hunched at the desk, almost within arm's reach.

With the hair at the back of his neck tingling, his breath tight in his lungs, he stepped cautiously into the corridor and flattened his back against the wall. First he looked to the left and into deeper shadows, then to the right and the pool of lamplight where Telfont labored with his scratching pen. As he watched, Telfont lifted his head and flexed his right arm several times as if it were cramped from writing so long. Then Telfont returned to his task. The pen scratched on.

As he pressed his shoulder blades hard against the wall, Lassiter saw or heard nothing suspicious.

Slowly he crept into the parlor to stand where the

light was dim, away from the glow of the single lamp where Telfont was scribbling away as if no one was within a mile of him.

"Careful, Telfont," Lassiter warned in a low voice.

Telfont's shoulders tightened and he straightened up slowly in his chair. He looked around at Lassiter standing in a shadowed corner of the large parlor. Thick carpets were scattered about the polished floor. Logs crackled in the big stone fireplace, the flames reflected in the polished brass at the mantel.

"Well, well, Lassiter," Telfont said with forced cheerfulness. "Guess I must have forgotten to lock the back door." He eyed the shotgun, licked his lips.

"Shut up and listen to me. You've got a man in this house. Tell him to show himself."

"And if I don't?"

"You'll be a greasespot on that chair."

Telfont looked again at the shotgun. His tongue flicked the underside of his thick mustache. "I paraded up and down in front of the windows on the chance you'd see me and figure to settle—"

"How'd you know I wouldn't shoot you through the window?"

"Because I know that's not the way you do things."

Quickly Lassiter crossed the room, got in behind Telfont and reached under the man's coat. He came up with a .45 with ebony grips. He tossed the weapon over his shoulder where it landed with a thud on the thick carpet.

"*Tell him to show himself!*" Lassiter repeated. "I'm talking about the other man in this house!"

Telfont's lips twisted in an ugly line across his

handsome face. He swallowed as the shotgun barrels touched his breastbone.

"Jud!" he cried hoarsely. "Where the hell are you? Get out here. But be careful, for crissakes. Lassiter's got that goddamned shotgun on me!"

There was the creaking sound of weight put on a loose board in the floor. Then the heavy laughter of Jud Ream. Lassiter's mouth dried and he flicked a glance in the direction of the laughter. He saw Ream looming up in the shadowed dining room that opened into the parlor.

Somehow Ivy Eading had entered the house. Her terrified eyes reflected the horror of her mistake. She was drawn with such force against Ream that her back was arched. One of Ream's hands was at her mouth. The other held a gun, its metal work touched by the faint light that reached the spot where the towering Ream and his captive had halted.

In Ream's massive hand, the gun looked like a toy. Its barrel dug cruelly into Ivy's throat.

Telfont spoke in a shaking voice. "Damn it, Jud, I told you to stay at my back." No man under the threat of a sawed-off shotgun could remain calm, not even Telfont.

"Seen a shadow move out back," Ream said through his large blunt teeth. "Knowed it wasn't big enough for Lassiter. So I moved quick. I got her. Was worth it, you ask me."

Telfont's forehead was slick with sweat. He got slowly to his feet and stood with both hands on the desk while he glared at Lassiter. "Yes, I guess maybe it was, Jud," he conceded. "Well, Lassiter? Stalemate?"

Lassiter stood rigidly, the shotgun still pointed at Telfont. He looked again at Ivy. Ream had removed his hand from her mouth, but his thick arm across her middle held her against him. A faint grin rode the mouth in the large, scarred face.

"You press those triggers," Telfont pointed out, his voice gaining strength, "and the girl will die. I don't think you're the kind to stand by while she gets a hole blown in her pretty throat."

"It is a stalemate," Lassiter said in that breathless moment. "Turn the girl loose and I'll back out of the house." It was pure bluff and Lassiter waited tensely to see if Telfont would take him up on it. He held his breath.

"Sure you can shoot me to rags," Telfont said with a vicious smile. "But the girl will be minus her head the minute you try for me." And as if on cue, Ream shifted the revolver muzzle from Ivy's throat to her left ear.

Lassiter saw the pallor of Ivy's face, saw her tremble as she was jammed back against Ream's big frame.

She looked imploringly at Lassiter. "I . . . I'm sorry. But I was worried about you. Go ahead, kill him, Lassiter." Her voice broke as Ream jerked his arm harder across her middle.

Ream's heavy chin rested atop her golden head. He was grinning as his big thumb drew back the hammer of his .45. The sound was ominous in the stillness with only the crackle of flames in the fireplace and Lassiter's own labored breathing to be heard.

"Lassiter, seems that you're like the wolf with his

hind leg caught in a bear trap. No matter how you figure it, you're dead," Ream said with a hard smile.

Lassiter debated, knowing that even if he risked one barrel of the shotgun and downed Telfont, then turned to Ream, he had no way of controlling the scythe of buckshot that would annihilate Ivy along with her captor.

"Jud's perfectly capable of killing the young lady," Telfont pointed out, faint impatience in his voice. He was leaning forward to peer at Lassiter's immobile features as if wondering if the man might take the risk after all.

Lassiter spoke in a voice thinned with tension. "Let her go. And I'll stay and face whatever comes next."

"No, Lassiter, no!" Ivy screamed. "Don't think of me!"

Ream shut her up by tightening his hold across her stomach, driving out her breath so that she would have folded over his thick arm had it not been for the gun at her ear. The pressure of the weapon tilted her head at an odd angle. Lassiter knew she was in pain.

"Give me your word that you'll let her go," Lassiter insisted to Telfont, but the man laughed.

"Put down the shotgun or she's dead."

Carefully Lassiter let down the twin hammers, stooped and placed the shotgun at his feet.

"Kick it over, Lassiter, along with that gun you've got stuck in your belt," Telfont ordered; he was once again in command.

Lassiter hesitated a second, then looked again at the girl in Ream's cruel grasp. The pain in her eyes was easy to read. He did as he was told. What choice did he have? he asked himself.

Telfont picked up the shotgun and the .45 and placed them on the mantel at his back, then got his own gun from the floor.

With Lassiter disarmed, Ream quickly walked Ivy to where Telfont was standing, keeping her bent backward and off balance and in no position to try and twist free.

Telfont pushed her into a chair. Then he told Ream to pull the drapes over the windows. "We don't want somebody seeing what goes on in here and butting in. Not until you're finished, Lassiter."

"What's going to happen to him?" Ivy wailed. She started to get out of the chair but Telfont shoved her back.

"Lassiter, you've bucked me all the way. But I'm willing to forget that if you tell me where you buried the Betain money."

"Let the girl get outside, goddammit, Telfont—"

Telfont's lips twisted. "You need a lesson. Go get him, Jud."

Grinning, Ream finished pulling the last of the drapes, then unbuckled his gunbelt. He placed it on the fireplace mantel beside the other .45 and the shotgun. One of the burning logs broke in two, sending a geyser of sparks up the chimney.

Ivy looked as if she was close to fainting. "Lassiter won't have a chance against that man," she gasped. That it was a mismatch was obvious. Lassiter was inches shorter and many pounds lighter.

Jud Ream's yellow eyes were contemptuous. "Lassiter, I always figured you had a soft spot in you big as an anvil. You just proved it by worryin' about the gal."

"Cold-blooded murder turns my stomach," Lassiter said and began to slide his boots over the polished floor. Ream was pushing up his shirtsleeves over forearms knotted with muscle. His wide chest seemed as impervious as an oak barrel. He spread his thick legs wide to give him balance. As Ream advanced, Lassiter could smell sweat and stale whiskey.

"Won't be no need to hang you," taunted Ream. "I'll hand the sheriff your head in a gunnysack."

"How brutal!" Ivy cried. Then she looked pleadingly up at Telfont who stood behind her chair. "Let him go. I'll do anything you want—"

"You will anyway, my dear." Telfont's laugh was unpleasant.

Lassiter felt his nerves tighten as he ducked away from the lash of a mighty left fist. Obviously Ream was toying with him, enjoying it. His thick lips were drawn back over his large teeth in a grin of anticipation.

"Too bad we ain't got a crowd to see this," Ream said.

"Lassiter, you've got one last chance. Tell me about the money," Telfont said angrily.

"Go to hell."

"Start in on him, Jud," Telfont snarled impatiently. "Don't forget I don't want him killed. Not until he tells me what I want to know."

Lassiter saw the right hand looming and twisted away, but it landed along the left side of his rib cage. He felt a stab of pain. His wound still gave him problems under stress. And stress he would have, a mountain of it with this monster.

He glanced at the shotgun and the .45 Telfont had placed on the mantel at his back. Telfont had re-

CHAPTER TWENTY-TWO

Before Lassiter could recover from the tremendous right he barely managed to avoid, and get his boots anchored solidly on the floor, Ream's heavy left smashed him in the face. Lassiter's head snapped back and he was aware that Ream's thick arms were encircling him. Desperately he squirmed free before they could lock into place around his torso.

Ream was big and he was tough and Lassiter knew he was giving away forty pounds in weight and at least three inches in height. As Lassiter broke free, Ream, with his longer reach, sent two solid blows to Lassiter's jaw. Lightning flashed in Lassiter's head and he gave ground rapidly, with Ream sliding ponderously across the polished floor after him.

Ivy was making sobbing protests to Telfont, who was staring in fascination at the combatants. There was a stillness in the big house with its draped parlor windows, golden lamplight reflecting on waxed paneling and chandelier filled with unlighted candles.

After two backing circuits of the room, dodging

furniture, keeping just out of Ream's extended reach, Lassiter's head began to clear. No longer did he see two Reams plodding after him. He suddenly stood his ground as Ream sprang forward, aiming a wild swing at the head. But Lassiter struck first, a savage blow to the midriff that doubled Ream up and brought a great gush of air laced with alcohol fumes from between his parted lips. With Ream bent over, gasping for breath, Lassiter moved in quickly for the kill.

But Telfont's harsh voice stopped him. "Hold it, Lassiter! Goddam it! Or I'll put a bullet in your leg! Jud, take a minute to get your breath."

Lassiter, breathing hard, turned his head from the stricken Ream to the cold muzzle of a revolver. And as he stared, Telfont pressed the gun under Ivy's left breast. A bullet into her heart if he didn't obey, said Telfont's vicious face.

Ream straightened up suddenly and said, "You won't do that again!" One of Lassiter's blows had peeled a strip of skin from Ream's cheekbone. Blood dripped down the thick neck and into the collar of his shirt.

When Ream charged again, Lassiter tried desperately to fight him off, but was pushed against a table next to the north wall. A glass bowl fell to the floor and rolled across the carpet, its prisms catching light from the fireplace.

Lassiter felt himself slammed even harder against the edge of the table as Ream leaned on him. But Lassiter fought back, landing short, telling jabs to the body. Ream wavered and Lassiter took heart. But the next instant Ream's desperation left crashed against Lassiter's jaw. In a moment of blackness, Lassiter knew he was falling.

Reaching out, he grabbed Ream around the knees and pulled him down. They crashed, then rolled apart. Lassiter got to his knees, his vision distorted, whirling into a kaleidoscope with its varied jangle of colored patterns.

Ream bounded to his feet with the grace of a puma. Lassiter was deliberately slower in getting up. He was vaguely aware of Ivy's groan of despair. But suddenly he came to life. On his feet, moving swiftly backward, he evaded Ream's rush. Ream muttered an oath and came charging in again, his heavy shoulders tightening a green shirt now speckled with his blood.

Each time Lassiter tried desperately to reach the mantel and get his hands on one of the weapons there, he was blocked either by Ream or Telfont, standing with one hand inside his coat, ready to draw his gun.

Lassiter whirled aside, letting Ream charge on past him. As Ream did so, Lassiter's right crashed into the big man's right side. A left flattened the tip of Ream's nose. Savage joy burst in Lassiter as Ream staggered. Ream tried to wipe the blood from his face with his forearm and at the same time keep out of Lassiter's reach.

"Get him down and tromp him!" Telfont shouted.

"That I'll do," was Ream's response as he roared in again, both fists swinging.

Lassiter blocked two blows, took another on the forehead that set up a clanging in his skull. With all his strength, Lassiter fought back. Sheer instinct enabled him to fight off Ream, his fists striking rhythmically.

Telfont yelled a faltering encouragement. "You got him now, Jud!"

The big man was reeling. He caught the heavy drapes at the side windows to give him balance and they ripped from their rod to crumple in heaps of red velvet on the floor. Lassiter's pursuit was relentless. Ream ducked and raced to the front windows where Lassiter trapped him. Again Ream used the window drapes for support, to pull himself up. But the drapes were ripped from their moorings. Moonlight poured into the parlor from the windows.

As Lassiter tried to reach the mantel, Ream's superior reach held him off. A whistling right slammed into Lassiter's breastbone.

Seeing that Ream had his back to Telfont, and that only a few feet separated the two men, Lassiter consolidated his waning powers into ponderous lefts and rights. Ream backed up, now off balance.

A shouted warning from Telfont. "Look out, Jud, for crissakes!"

And Telfont was forced to duck aside to avoid Ream's flailing arms as the man attempted to retain his balance. Telfont, bent over, was trying to push Ivy away at the same time.

Seeing his chance, Lassiter spun away from Ream, seized Telfont's right wrist and twisted free the gun he had been holding on Ivy.

"Run!" Lassiter shouted at her. *"Run!"*

And run she did, scampering out of Telfont's reach. Ream at the same time tried to wrap his arms around Lassiter and bring him down. Lassiter was desperately backing away, trying to get enough room to bring into play the revolver he had seized from Telfont.

One of Ream's clubbed fists struck Lassiter's right wrist with such force that the gun was knocked from his grasp. As it skidded along the floor, Lassiter dived for it, but Ream caught his ankle and pulled him away.

Ivy was outside, screaming into the darkness, "Help, help! They're trying to beat Lassiter to death. I lied . . . Lassiter didn't kill Betain . . . !"

Lassiter failed to hear more. Kicking free of Ream's grasp on his ankle, he leaped to his feet. As Ream drew back his right fist to end it all, Lassiter struck first. It seemed to him that his succeeding blows were about as effective as hammering against a barn wall with his fists. Gradually he became aware that Ream was staggering, gasping and uttering groans from the gut. Lassiter saw the wild, red-rimmed eyes, the blood streaming from the many deep facial cuts, the mouth twisted in pain. Lassiter's left struck the mid-section with such force that Ream's torso flipped downward as if on a giant hinge.

And as the face came down, Lassiter's right was lifting. He felt his knuckles land solidly against the shelf of jaw. Ream's knees caved in and he pawed the air. Lassiter, breathing hard, stepped back, allowing the man to fall facedown, making the floor shake. Ream's legs flipped up, then settled.

Telfont had snatched up the .45 from the mantel and gone charging after Ivy, but she had a headstart and was too swift. She was still screaming somewhere outside in the darkness.

Winded as he was, Lassiter started to stagger

across the room toward Telfont's revolver, a dull gleam in the corner of the oversize room. Then in his befuddled state he saw the butt of the shotgun protruding from the edge of the high mantel.

As he veered in that direction, Telfont came rushing back into the room. He saw Lassiter's move and fired. The bullet ricocheted off one of the stones of the fireplace. As it went screaming away, Telfont ducked out of sight in a hallway.

Lassiter paused for breath, the shotgun pointed at the spot where he had last seen Telfont. He heard Ivy's voice out in the yard, then heard boots hammering the veranda steps. The front door flung open.

Joe Gilbey was first into the house, followed by Red Shanley with his blotched skin and fiery red hair. Behind him was the shabbily dressed Jethro, who had been a party to Telfont's plan to get Doc Maydon out of the way. A big pistol was gripped in his grimy hand.

All three men came up short to stare at Ream who lay with his beaten face turned to one side. They didn't see Lassiter who had backed to the far end of the room in the shadows where the lamplight did not quite reach. . . .

CHAPTER TWENTY-THREE

Telfont's strident voice came from the security of the darkened hallway. *"Get Lassiter! But watch it, he's got the shotgun . . . !"*

Lassiter had been leaning against the wall to give support to his shaky knees. But now he swung away to face this new danger. Gilbey was already firing at the spot where Lassiter had been but an instant before. Bullets laced the wall. As Gilbey shifted his aim to make the necessary corrections, Lassiter touched the back trigger of the shotgun. In the roar and scythe of metal that erupted from the barrel, Gilbey was thrown backward and to the floor, his perforated midsection already staining his clothing. Red Shanley took a few of the pellets himself. But not enough to spoil his aim. A firebrand creased Lassiter's neck. He felt the shock of it to his toes, felt the warmth of his own blood.

But this time he aimed more carefully, not wishing even now to repeat the horror of Joe Gilbey, who had been nearly cut in two. He fired the remaining barrel of the shotgun into Shanley's legs. Mingled with the explosion and belch of smoke was Shanley's scream of pain.

By then Jethro had plunged out through the open front door, screaming, "He's got a shotgun!"

There were the sounds of men approaching, and Ivy's shrill voice as she tried to explain something. But Lassiter only barely heard her above the hubbub. He clenched his teeth against the pain of his neck wound. Throwing aside the empty shotgun, he picked up from the floor the revolver taken from Telfont that Ream had knocked out of his hand. His fingers closed on the ebony gun grips.

Lassiter's body was one solid ache from the furious pounding of Ream's fists. Blood was soaking into his shirt. His head felt light. But his brain wasn't dulled. In him was the certainty that if he failed to end it now, Telfont would be the victor.

"Telfont!" came Lassiter's loud challenge. "Let's settle it, man to man. If you've got the guts!"

In the yard there was sudden silence. Telfont filled the void. "Nothing I'd like better, Lassiter. Come outside."

"I'm coming out. With my hands lifted. You kill me and it'll be murder!"

"Oh, I intend to give you a fair shake," Telfont drawled loudly from somewhere out in the darkness.

Lassiter was aware of the dead silence. He started for the front door where Telfont had vanished onto the veranda. Then Lassiter halted, turned his head. In the light spilling from the downstairs parlor windows and the few lanterns held high out in the yard, Lassiter glimpsed Telfont. He saw him through a window, standing a dozen feet down the veranda, eyes riveted on the front doorway, legs widespread, arms loose at his sides.

Behind Telfont was a cleared space but in the yard were perhaps two dozen men, with more running up from the main part of town.

"I'm coming out, Telfont!" Lassiter called. "Watch it!"

"Out with your hands in the air. I'm waiting. We'll get somebody to count to ten, then we'll go at it!"

"Fair enough!"

Lassiter took several deep breaths to quiet his nerves, then lifted his hands and moved toward the front door. He reached it, started through, only the slack in his shirt front showing. Then something made him pull back sharply. A gun crashed. A bullet was buried into the door frame. Flying splinters cut into Lassiter's right cheek.

A man roared from the yard, "Telfont, that was a sneak trick!"

"Since when does a condemned murderer have any rights?" Telfont demanded.

"The young lady here has been filling our ears," shouted Teeley of the saloon.

"She's a liar!" Telfont challenged.

"Maybe not—"

"She's warmed many a blanket in her young lifetime. Including mine! She's not fit—"

Out in the yard Teeley cupped hands to his mouth so his shout would carry. "Lassiter, can you hear me?"

"Yeah, I hear you!"

"Give yourself up. We'll get to the bottom of this. If you're not guilty—"

Telfont interrupted with a wild laugh. "Hell with

that, Teeley. He murdered my friend, Joe Gilbey. He'll pay for that. I've got my own brand of justice!"

Then there was the sound of Telfont running down the long veranda, away from the entry. In a few seconds the rear door where Ream had entered with Ivy creaked open. Telfont moved at a crouch along the hall toward the parlor.

"Holster your gun and I'll do likewise," Lassiter started to say, but Telfont laughed.

A bullet slammed into the paneling at Lassiter's back. He was wheeling to make himself a poor target, firing at the gun flashes. He missed. But when he came full around and met Telfont's bared teeth at twenty feet and snapped the hammer, nothing happened. Only a dry click issued from the first of the weapons Lassiter had grabbed during his wild escape from jail.

Seeing Lassiter's predicament, Telfont straightened from his crouch, a grin stretching his mustache. His once handsome face was now taut with tension and uncertainty.

In that space of seconds, Lassiter flung himself to the floor in desperation, his right arm outflung toward the gun Red Shanley had dropped when shot through the legs.

Telfont's gun crashed, its bullet cutting a long groove in the oak floor only inches from Lassiter's nose. As Lassiter rolled to a sitting position, his heart seemed too tight for his rib cage. He was halfway expecting to be blasted from the face of the earth. Both guns exploded simultaneously. But there was a fraction of difference. And that fraction knocked Telfont down, squirming on the floor, while his bullet took out a front window. Out in the yard and on the veranda there was much yelling as men fought to get out of the line of fire.

Lassiter got shakily to his feet. Blood from the deep gash on his neck had run down his side, soaking his shirt, and the waistband of his canvas work pants. Lights danced in his head. The pain from the wound was like a knife blade in the flesh.

Breathing hard, Lassiter walked over and reached to catch Telfont by an arm and pull him, sagging, into a sitting position.

"Tell 'em, Telfont!" Lassiter put power into his voice. "Tell 'em how you brought in those two card sharps to trim Betain. Tell 'em how you found Betain wounded after he shot me. And how I was lucky enough to put a bullet in him. Tell 'em how you finished Betain off!"

Lassiter was clutching at straws because he didn't know all the details for sure. But he could tell from the change in Telfont's bloodshot eyes that he had scored. Telfont looked up from the floor where he sagged. Lassiter still gripped him by the arm. Telfont's amber gaze reflected pain from a nasty looking hole on the left side of his chest that bubbled red with each heartbeat. His face was graying.

"You're about done for, Telfont!" Lassiter yelled, hoping to get it over with at last. Men had crowded around to stare. Among them stood a grim-looking Sheriff McKenzie. He was bareheaded. There was dried blood at the back of his head where Lassiter had been forced to strike him down. What could be seen of his face in the full beard was nearly as pale as Telfont's.

"Speak up, Telfont," McKenzie urged in a harsh voice.

Telfont rolled his eyes as if assessing the possibility of friendly faces. But there seemed to be none.

"The girl's already told me plenty," McKenzie said sternly.

"Stand back," Telfont gasped, gesturing with his right hand; Lassiter still gripped his left arm. "Give me air. I . . . I'll talk . . ."

"Do like he says, Lassiter." McKenzie got a grip on Lassiter's wrist and pulled him back.

And it was then that Lassiter was aware of the imminence of death. Something in Telfont's eyes alerted him, a sudden spark of determination replacing the fading light. In his muddled state, Lassiter had neglected a cardinal rule: no matter how badly wounded the enemy might be, search him for a hideout always. Do that first before anything else.

In the space of three heartbeats he had seen Telfont fumble under his coat as if to feel of his wound. But instead, his hand came into view, a wicked-looking derringer locked in his fingers, a two-shot, one barrel above the other.

"You son of a bitch, Lassiter," Telfont suddenly screeched, as men, yelling, dived for cover. "You spoiled it all. I'll take you with me, by Christ if I won't . . . !"

Lassiter was diving, not away from Telfont but toward him, to try and get a hand on that derringer before some innocent bystander was cut down. But even as he was in midair, he knew he'd never reach it. He fully expected it to be the last act of his life, that one of those bullets from the hideout derringer would tear into his face.

At the last possible moment he was flinging himself aside. A twitching of the long black hair at the crown of his head told him how close the bullet had come. He heard the roar of the small weapon, felt the bite of gunsmoke in his nostrils. Somehow he retained his grip on the weapon he had taken earlier from Shanley. He came down hard on his left elbow, felt a knifing pain. Before Telfont could shift the derringer for another shot, Lassiter thumbed a bullet directly between the man's glittering eyes. Telfont slumped full length on the floor, the light already fading from his eyes.

Since Doc Maydon's death, there was no doctor in town, but Ella Ormsby had acquired a rudimentary knowledge of medicine over the years by assisting Maydon. First she picked buckshot out of Red Shanley's legs, then cleansed and bandaged Lassiter's neck wound. Just as she was finishing, Ivy Eading came through the crowd gathered in front of the late doctor's house.

She had repeated her story to the judge. Red Shanley, begging for mercy, had verified it along with Jethro. All charges against Lassiter were dismissed.

Ivy was returning to the Beauchamp Store in Tucson, the only home she knew. Smiling shyly, she gave Lassiter a slip of paper with the name written on it. "Maybe one day you'll stop by."

Then she was gone. He called to her and tried to get to his feet, but his legs were too wobbly.

Later that day, the ranchers and their families, who had come so far for the hanging, watched him solemnly as he rode out with Victoria Reed at his side.

"Reckon I spoiled their fun," Lassiter said with a wry grin and shook his head.

"No matter what," Victoria said firmly, the sunlight touching red-gold hair showing under her hat brim, "I was determined to get you out of that jail."

"Likely you'd have only gotten yourself shot, or killed."

"I was willing to take that chance. I was working on it when I heard that you'd broken out. It was the best news I ever heard in my life."

As they rode toward Plato Mine, taking it easy because of his wound, he told her about the money Xavier Betain had sent for his son. "As Corse Betain's widow, the money's yours."

"For the two of us, then," she said hopefully.

After he got his strength back in a few days, he'd dig it up for her. "Less two thousand dollars the old man promised me," he added with a tight smile.

"Take it all, Lassiter, every dollar. God knows you've earned it." But he was adamant on that subject.

Before the week was out they learned that Telfont's assets, stolen from stockholders with the aid of a pair of card sharks, had been located at a bank in an adjoining county. It was judged to be the property of said stockholders in the Sunrise Valley Railroad—not only the money, but all the property Telfont had acquired in Sunrise.

"I'll put some of my late father-in-law's money into the railroad," Victoria said excitedly, "and use the rest to start the mine operating again. If you'll help me run it."

Her gray eyes lost their sparkle when he shook his head. "What you need is a mining man. Not a drifter like me."

"But I want a drifter like you!" she exclaimed.

In the end, Lassiter won out. He located a mining man, Seth Harkness, personable, in his thirties, who had lost his wife and decided it was time to rejoin the world after a period of mourning.

One morning in early summer, Lassiter headed south. On the way he looked at the slip of paper Ivy had given him, with directions to the Beauchamp Store. Well, why not? He'd stop in on his way and say howdy. One thing Ivy had learned, he was sure, was that hatred and a burning desire for vengeance can sometimes twist the soul and turn the world ugly. . . .

LOREN ZANE GREY

A GRAVE FOR LASSITER

Even before his adventures in *Riders of the Purple Sage*, Lassiter was regarded as the mightiest gunslinger ever to sit a saddle. Therefore, it's no surprise he's the first man Josh Falconer calls to help save his business from the local tough trying to bankrupt his freight line. Though when Lassiter arrives in Bluegate, Josh is already dead and he finds his worst enemy, Kane Farrell, set to take over the line. With a price on his head, Lassiter doesn't get far before he's ambushed, shot and left for dead. But even death won't get in the way of his vengeance. He's determined the only man needing a grave will be Farrell.

LOREN ZANE GREY
AMBUSH FOR LASSITER

Framed for a murder they didn't commit, Lassiter and his best pal Borling are looking at twenty-five years of hard time in the most notorious prison of the West. In a daring move, they make a break for freedom—only to be double-crossed at the last minute. Lassiter ends up in solitary confinement, but Borling takes a bullet to the back. When at last Lassiter makes it out, there's only one thing on his mind: vengeance.

WILL HENRY

BLIND CAÑON

In the midst of the Alaskan gold rush, Murrah Starr holds a rich claim that should set him up for life. Trouble is, his life may be a lot shorter than he'd like. Starr is a half-breed Sioux whose only friend is a wolf dog he once freed from a trap. Angus McClennon, the head of the local miners' association, is dead set on taking Starr's claim for himself. First he spearheads a law that declares only American citizens can own a mine. Then a group of miners beat Starr and leave him for dead in the middle of the street. But Starr is just as determined as McClennon. He's determined to fight for what's his—and to stay alive while doing it!

BLOOD BROTHERS

COTTON SMITH

Former Texas Ranger John Checker is ready to go home to Dodge City. He and his friends have survived—barely—a bloody battle with Checker's half-brother, Star McCallister, and his gang. But heading home and getting there alive are two different things. They have some mighty dangerous territory to cross first, and McCallister has his own plans for Checker…plans that involve two hired killers.

KITT PEAK

AL SARRANTONIO

Retirement does not agree with former lieutenant Thomas Mullin. So when he receives a whiskey-stained letter detailing the disappearance of his friend's daughter Abby, he jumps on the first train to Arizona. Folks around town think Abby has gone back to the reservation where she was raised, yet the more Mullin investigates, the more suspicious he becomes. But even his agile mind and gift for deduction can't prepare him for the wild legends of the Papagos or the terrifying truth of what's really in store for Abby.

- -

RIDERS OF
THE PURPLE SAGE
ZANE GREY®

Zane Grey's masterpiece, *Riders of the Purple Sage*, is one of the greatest, most influential novels of the West ever written. But for nearly a century it has existed only in a profoundly censored version, one that undermined the truth of the characters and distorted Grey's intentions.

Finally the story has been restored from Grey's original handwritten manuscript and the missing and censored material has been reinserted. At long last the classic saga of the gunman known only as Lassiter and his search for his lost sister can be read exactly as Zane Grey wrote it. After all these years, here is the **real** *Riders of the Purple Sage*!